BET
ON ICE

BET ON ICE

BOYS OF WINTER #9

S.R. GREY

Bet on Ice (Boys of Winter #9)
Copyright © 2020 by S.R. Grey

ISBN-13 (print edition): 978-0-9601037-3-7

Editing: Hot Tree Editing
Proofreading: Deaton Author Services
Beta Readers: Franci N. and JoAnna E.
Cover Photographer: Wander Aguiar Photography
Model: Braun Wilburn
Cover Design: Najla Qamber
Formatting: E.M. Tippetts

OTHER BOOKS BY
S.R. GREY

A Harbour Falls Mystery trilogy
Harbour Falls
Willow Point
Wickingham Way

Laid Bare novella series
Exposed: Laid Bare 1
Unveiled: Laid Bare 2
Spellbound: Laid Bare 3
Sacrifice: Laid Bare 4

1

WANNA BET, SWEETHEART?

LANDEN

Smiling smugly, I flip my cards over.

I have two jacks—that's twenty.

Yes!

I beat the dealer. She has only seventeen. And my teammates, who are playing blackjack with me tonight, are out of the game, having just laid down their shitty hands.

Brimming with confidence, I reach for the mountain of chips in the middle of the gaming table.

But as I move the pile an inch or so closer, the pretty woman on my right, the very one who's been handing me my ass all night, clears her throat.

I pause, my arms outstretched, still on my loot.

Glancing over at her annoyedly, I say, "Yes?"

"Uh, uh, uh," she tsks, waving her finger. "Not so fast there,

Blondie."

Blondie?

Who in the hell does this chick think she is?

For starters, her hair is far blonder than mine. I'm dishwater; she's honey and sunshine.

Her hair is also much longer.

And so damn shiny too…

Stop!

Shaking my head, I tear my gaze from her pretty locks.

It shouldn't bother me that she's been calling me Blondie for the past hour, ever since my teammates and I first sat down at this table.

Never mind I've told her twice my name is Landen.

She obviously doesn't care.

Fine, whatever.

She clearly has no idea she's playing cards with three of the best players on the Las Vegas Wolves hockey team.

I actually kind of like that, though.

It's better than the alternative—getting fawned over for being a professional sports player, having to sign autographs, plastering on a fake smile for selfies, and on and on.

You get the picture, right?

So yeah, anonymity is refreshing, especially since we're playing in a back room of a well-known casino on the famous Las Vegas Strip.

Lying low is of paramount importance, even though it's not real busy tonight in the private VIP area.

That's a bonus.

And it makes me think…

How did this pretty woman next to me, the one who insists on calling me Blondie, end up here tonight. This room is reserved for high rollers and premier card players. My teammates and I come here because we like that they play a version of blackjack where both cards dealt to each player remain down.

It adds intrigue to the game.

Maybe this chick likes that too.

She was seated at the table already when Nolan Solvenson, Benny Perry, and I first arrived.

As we took our seats, she was chatting with the dealer. There were no other players at that point, so it wasn't like she could play.

Speaking of the dealer, she's cute too. She has dark brunette hair, cut in a pixie style, and deep brown eyes.

I noticed her as soon as we sat down.

But my attention was quickly averted to my card nemesis.

She is fucking hot as sin.

I'd be a lot angrier losing to her if she wasn't so damn sexy. The short, siren-red skintight dress she's wearing is unbelievable, and her toned long legs might be the death of me before this night ends.

I look up at her from what I think is a sly perusal only to realize I've been busted.

"Shit," I murmur.

My card nemesis raises a perfectly arched brow, and it's then that I notice her eyes are as stunning as she is.

They're this cool blue, azure like the sea.

While I'm drowning in their depths, the gorgeous woman smirks.

She then makes a show of flipping her cards over.

Fuck, she has a jack and an ace.

"Twenty-one," the dealer with the pixie cut declares, like we can't all fucking see that.

"Yeah, yeah, yeah, what-the-fuck-ever," I grumble as I push the chips over to my nemesis.

"Why, thank you, Landen," she coos, stacking her take alongside her already formidable pile of chips.

"Ahh, so you do remember my name," I say, chuckling.

"Of course, I remember, *Landen.*"

Smartass.

"Could've fooled me," I mumble.

She hears me and laughs.

Good, laugh now.

This battle is on.

When I glance her way again, she's peering over at me curiously, her brow furrowed, azure eyes troubled.

Have I been had?

No, I don't think so.

This feels more like she's deciding on something.

Or maybe she knows some tidbit I don't.

Yeah, like what cards are coming up next.

This chick is that damn good.

It's like she's the dude from *Rainman* or something.

Though I guess she'd be *Rainwoman*, right?

Ah hell, it doesn't matter.

Suddenly and surprising the shit out of me, she holds out her hand and says very nicely, "I'm Cricket, by the way."

This is the friendliest and most genuine she's been all night.

Too bad I can't help but laugh in her face.

Her eyes flash in anger.

There goes our tentative truce.

I'm in for it now, so I may as well head straight to Hell.

As I wrap my large hand around her dainty one, I snort. "Cricket, eh? What kind of name is that? Was your father or mother an entomologist?"

Cricket yanks her hand back like I just burned her.

I guess, in a way, I have.

Sniffing, she snaps, "For your information, Cricket is a good name. It's a fun one too. It's also the name my mother gave me twenty-four years ago. And no, neither of my parents are entomologists. Not that I owe you any kind of an explanation, jackass."

"Ooh, burn," Benny interjects.

I ignore him and say to Cricket, "True, you don't owe me an explanation. But you sure as hell just gave me one."

That angers her further.

Man, I'm a jerk.

I don't know why I'm doing this.

"Have I told you that I hate you?" Cricket grinds out.

Crap, now I feel bad.

"Ah, come on. I'm just yanking your chain. You know, having a little fun?" With my best *mea culpa* smile in play—and it usually is pretty dazzling—I add, "I actually agree that Cricket is a good name. A damn good one."

"You got that right," she huffs.

And then, finally, she begins to relax.

See, my smile works every time.

I even catch her trying to hide a bit of a grin. A real one too, not a snotty smirk, like the ones she's been doling out in our interactions.

I think I may be growing on her.

I may be "growing" like a fungus, but hey, I'll take what I can get.

Out of the blue, and rather obnoxiously, Nolan, seated on my left, asks loudly, "Are you two in on this next game or not? I mean, hell, I hate to intrude on your googly eyes and flirting, but let's get this show on the road."

"We're not flirting," Cricket snaps, narrowing her eyes over at Nolan. "I don't even like this guy."

Now it's my turn to be appalled.

"Wait, what? What do you mean you don't like me?"

Snorting and turning away, she says, "I don't. It's pretty simple, genius. For someone who knows words like 'entomologist,' you sure are dumb."

"Heyyy," I protest.

Nolan, chuckling, snipes, "Yeah, sure you don't like him. What a crock. Pull this leg and it plays 'Jingle Bells.'"

"I don't even know what that means," Cricket says, looking confused as hell.

"Never mind," I tell her. Cupping my hand to the side of my mouth to address only her, I quietly add, "Just ignore him. We all do."

Benny, over on Nolan's other side, has been laughing like crazy throughout this whole exchange.

While the dealer just waits patiently.

Yeah, you don't rush high rollers.

She knows the deal.

Leaning across the table, Benny then says to Cricket, "It's a holiday saying, the 'Jingle Bells' comment. Since yesterday was Christmas and all, Nolan, is apparently feeling extra festive."

All three of us crack up then, and Cricket, rightfully so, mutters under her breath, "You're all a bunch of assholes."

In this circumstance, we are.

We deserve her ire.

"So," Nolan begins once we've composed ourselves, "are we playing cards or not?"

I hold up a hand. "Yes, we're playing. I'm in."

"I'm in too," Cricket states defiantly.

Whoa, she's scowling hard over at Nolan.

Not that he notices. He's too busy telling the dealer, "We're ready."

She begins passing out the cards, and Cricket directs her attention to her hand.

I do the same, and we make our bets.

Cricket goes all in.

She didn't start with a lot, but she's won so much that her pot is currently huge.

I try to assess if she's bluffing or not now for this hand.

I don't know, though. She has a good poker face.

Oooh, but wait, maybe not so much at this moment.

With the way that she's trying to hide a smile, those cards must be fucking awesome…again.

Too bad I'm grinning like a mofo too.

That's right, bitches—I have a king and an eight.

Not too shabby.

I go all in, as well.

Since I like to live a little dangerously—you should see me out on the ice—I say to the dealer, "Hit me."

She slides me another card, face down.

Grimacing and holding my breath, I take a quick peek.

Holy shit, it's a three.

With my king and an eight, I have fucking twenty-one.

Cricket can't beat this.

I hold, as does she, while Benny and Nolan ask for so many cards that they end up going over and folding.

Not me, though.

And I know for sure I've won this round when the dealer flips her cards and has only nineteen.

"Who's the fucking man?" I mutter under my breath.

Cricket, hearing that, says, "Not you. The more appropriate statement in this circumstance is 'Who's the fucking woman,' as I so have this."

I chortle. "Wanna bet, sweetheart?"

Cricket cocks her head, and damn, she really is one spectacular woman.

And I am one smitten fool.

"So," she says slowly, "by 'wanna bet,' do you mean you'd like to make a side wager? If so, I'm up for one."

Ah, a woman after my own heart.

I think I may be in love.

Okay, not love, but definitely in lust.

Nodding, I reply, "Now that you mention it, I do mean exactly that."

"Okay, sure, let's do it. And since I know I'm going to win, you don't even have to tell me what you want for our little side wager. How do you like that?"

"I like it," I say. "Don't bother telling me what you want, either."

"I won't." She smiles smugly. "This is going to be so much fun, watching you lose."

"That's not happening," I declare as I flip my cards over with complete confidence.

Not missing a beat, Cricket does the same with her own cards.

We both look down at the same time.

Yes!

She has two queens—that's twenty.

It's not enough.

"I won," I declare. "Just like I told you I would."

She rolls her eyes, muttering, "Whatever."

Reaching forward, I haul in the chips.

And this time they really are all mine.

With her beautiful full lips poised in a sexy pout, Cricket asks, "So what do I owe you for our side bet?"

"That's easy." I smile over at her. "Just go out with me."

Her eyes widen. "Like what? On a date?"

I laugh. "Exactly like on a date, yes."

Why does she look so uneasy all of a sudden?

Frowning, she says, "Okay, I'll give you my number. But can we make a final decision on this date thing tomorrow?"

Huh?

This is weird.

"Tomorrow? Er, uh, I guess. Why do we have to wait, though? Are you married and your divorce becomes final at midnight or something?"

"No," she states quietly, "it's nothing like that."

"Well, that's good to know," I mutter.

Still, I am so confused.

Cricket pulls out a pen and a slip of paper from her purse and jots down her phone number.

As she hands me the paper, she says, "Trust me on this waiting thing. It really is for the best."

What choice do I have?

Shaking my head, thinking Cricket sure is one hot mess, I tell her, "Sure. We can play this however you want."

We can too, however bizarre it's all become.

I have no idea why, either.

Guess I'll just have to wait and find out tomorrow.

MIXING BUSINESS WITH PLEASURE

CRICKET

*O**h, hell! What did I just do?**

Ugh, I know what I did. I foolishly made a wager with freaking Landen Zehner, and now the big beautiful blond left winger for the Las Vegas Wolves wants to go out with me on a date.

Not that I'm averse to the idea, as he is beyond hot.

Oh, and by the way, I know all about him. Pretending that I didn't was just an act.

Landen is twenty-six and a relatively new arrival to Las Vegas. He was traded to the Wolves from the Islanders this past summer. He's a forward who plays left wing and is friends with right winger Blake Cavaletti, another fairly new Wolves acquisition who plays on his line.

Other facts I know about Landen are that he's not married or currently involved with anyone, nor does he have kids.

I've also heard he's a bit of a bad boy.

I like the bad boy part.

Landen is my kind of guy.

Oh, and I certainly don't "not" like him.

That was an act as well.

Kind of like me pretending I didn't know I was playing cards with three hot and sexy Wolves players.

It was all just a ploy to lie low.

I saw no reason to stroke their already big egos.

So I chose to let them think I was clueless about who they are and what they do for a living.

It's funny that since I was at the VIP table, they probably assume I'm some kind of a high roller.

That makes me laugh, as it couldn't be further from the truth.

I was only in that back room because I'm friends with the blackjack dealer, Bettina. She and I went to graduate school together. I finished my MBA seven months ago, back in May.

Bettina, though, has one more semester to go.

The money she makes dealing cards in the back room of one of the biggest casinos on the Strip helps pay her way.

"Enough about Bettina," I murmur as I pull up to my townhouse on the west side of Vegas. "Let's get back to Landen."

Yes, let's.

It's amusing that he thinks I have no idea who he is. Too bad he doesn't know it's my business to learn all I can about the Wolves players.

See, I just landed a sweet job in marketing as their team's event coordinator.

That's right—I'm newly employed by the very same team Landen plays for.

So yeah, I'm aware of the players.

I know their names, faces, and bios.

I better.

My first promotional event is tomorrow afternoon.

And guess who it's with?

Yep, you guessed it—Landen.

I chuckle as I walk up to my townhouse, pressing the button on the key fob to lock my car, a simple silver hybrid sedan.

Tomorrow should be interesting, to say the least.

Landen Zehner has no clue that when he shows up at the arena in twelve short hours to skate with a group of school kids, I'll be the point person he'll be working with.

That's why I asked him to wait to decide if he still wants to go out with me.

It's only fair.

Though the Wolves have no restrictions or rules in place addressing dating amongst players and team employees—trust me, I've read that rulebook a dozen times—a lot of guys still don't like to mix business with pleasure.

I need to find out where Landen stands on that issue before we move forward.

As I walk into my empty, quiet home, flipping on the lights, I note how fresh and new it still smells, like latex paint, recently installed carpeting, and newly bought furniture.

It should smell this way, as I've only owned the townhouse since September. And even though it's pretty far out from the city, it came with a hefty mortgage.

That is why I better do a stellar job with the Wolves.

I need this job.

As I place my purse on the sofa in the living room, I look up at the darkness visible through the skylights and think about how I hope Landen doesn't care about the whole mixing business and pleasure thing.

Damn it, I really do want to go out with the guy.

I guess it's because I'm über attracted to him.

But he sure doesn't need to know that.

No way.

I'll continue to play it cool, like I did at the card game.

Yeah, let him wonder what I'm thinking.

Hockey boys are far too cocky, Landen included. I've read about his wild days. Though, to his credit, word is that he's settled down a lot since then.

Like me, he even bought a house recently.

As I glance around, I think about how his place is probably much bigger and fancier.

Me, I was just excited to have two whole bedrooms and a bath and a half to call my own.

Woohoo!

Despite his recent settling down in some ways, I think Landen has a lot of wildness left in him. He's a madman on the ice, taking chances with the puck and standing up to players much bigger than himself all the time.

And then there's the fact I saw something in his pretty sage green eyes tonight, something untamed.

I groan.

Why do I like that in my men?

I guess I'm into wild.

No, there's no use pretending.

I freaking love wild and untamed!

Landen could use a little domesticating, though…from me.

Good thing I'm the kind of girl who can get it done.

And if Landen falls for me in the process?

Well then, so be it.

I wouldn't be sad.

No way.

I'd be elated.

Kicking off my heels, I hike up my red dress, plop down on the sofa, and make a little wager with myself.

"I bet I can make Landen fall for me."

I don't mean in some trivial, lustful way, either.

I want him head over heels.

I think about what I'd gain if that were to happen.

That's an easy one—I'd win him.

And, no doubt about it, Landen Zehner would be quite the prize.

3

HOLY SHIT!

LANDEN

I wake up the morning after the blackjack game to the sound of lawn equipment whirring out on my property.

"Ah, hell," I mutter. "I forgot the landscapers were coming today."

I recently bought a newly constructed home that's kind of off the beaten path.

I like that.

I'm not a suburbs guy, so it's great to have a lot of land.

Unfortunately, though, thanks to the desert climate and constant beating sun, the lush green lawn and many shrubs and flowers I had put in need frequent watering and tending.

As if to remind me of that, a weed whacker just down from my bedroom window starts buzzing incessantly.

Annnd there goes all hope of going back to sleep.

So much for getting in a little extra rest after being out so late last night.

Sighing, I swing my legs over the edge of the mattress and sit up.

Running my hand down my stubbled face, I yawn and stretch and mutter, "Fuck, I'm tired."

I know a long hot shower will revive me, so I stand and head to the en suite bathroom.

I sleep in the nude, so there's no need to ditch any pajamas.

When I feel a familiar tug in my groin and glance down, I see that I'm sporting some pretty impressive morning wood.

Chuckling, I think, *I should take care of that.*

Yeah, no, I definitely will.

I know just who to fantasize about too—the beautiful, hot, and sexy woman I met last night, Cricket.

"I hope she decides to go out with me," I murmur as I step into the shower and turn on the water.

As jets blast me from multiple angles, I think about how weird it is that Cricket wants to wait to see if I would still like to go out with her.

Why wait till today?

It's all so strange.

"Whatever."

I have too many other things on my mind right now, first of which is getting to work on my raging hard-on.

Closing my eyes, I reach down and hit Play on this morning's fantasy, starring Cricket…

Shit, she's wearing that hot-as-sin red dress, and my hands are on her soft thighs, hiking the material up, up, up.

Yeah, we didn't part ways in the back room. We came here to my house afterward. And now we're in my bedroom, mere inches from the king-sized bed where I plan to do a lot of very dirty things to her.

Filthy, even.

"Unh, yeah…"

I stroke harder and faster.

Cricket's not wearing any panties, and she's already so fucking wet and ready for me. I dip a finger into her soaked pussy, quickly adding two more when she moans and begs for that.

"Stretch me out," she says. "Make me ready for your big, hard cock."

I like the way she thinks.

As I pump into her, she gasps out my name.

Damn, I can't hold out much longer.

I need to taste her, so I pull my fingers out and lick them.

Watching me, Cricket squirms, begging now for my tongue.

"Your wish is my command," I groan in real life as I lean back against the rough stone wall.

In my fantasy, I drop down to my knees.

I start licking and savoring her folds, parting her wide.

She has the sweetest, pinkest pussy I've ever tasted or seen.

I must have her.

Standing, I lower Cricket down to the bed.

Plunging into her in my fantasy makes me explode into my hand.

In real life, I'd last much longer.

Today is simply about taking care of business.

Once my heart rate returns to normal, I clean up and get on with showering.

As I'm soaping up, I think about how I'm hoping more than ever now that Cricket goes out with me.

I'd love to bring the fantasy I just had to life.

I still don't fully understand the "wait till tomorrow" crap, but whatever.

Tomorrow is here, and I have her number.

I'll see how things proceed and make a move from there.

Should I be looking for signs?

What kind, though.

Oh, hell, I'll just call her later to find out if I passed whatever "wait till tomorrow" test there was.

I'm glad I have a promo event at noon. It'll keep me busy. I won't obsess too much about Cricket and her weird stipulation to our bet.

For this event, I'll be skating with a group of kids from a disadvantaged school.

I love that the Wolves do shit like this, helping in the community and all.

Working with kids is the best. They're always so excited to skate with a real professional hockey player. Today should be even more special, as I get to surprise the kids with a donation of a bunch of brand-new hockey equipment, enough to start a team of their own at their school.

The Wolves covered about half the cost, and I kicked in the rest.

I like giving back.

I'm all about paying it forward.

After I'm showered, I dress in dark wash jeans and a red-and-black Wolves tee. Downstairs in the kitchen, I grab a quick breakfast of juice, fruit, and a few hard-boiled eggs.

I'm feeling pretty chill, until I'm on my way to the arena and realize I have no idea whom I'm meeting with today to find out about how this thing will run.

Crap.

I have no clue.

There's always a point person, an event coordinator, but the Wolves lost the guy who used to do this kind of thing. He moved to another state right before Christmas.

The team must've filled the job, though, right?

Otherwise, they would've postponed the event.

Now that I think about it, I do recall, in a recent email correspondence, there was mention of a new event coordinator who would be on hand.

Ah, so I'm in luck.

But, shit, I should've asked what his—or her—name is.

Hell, it doesn't matter.

I'll find out soon enough, as I just pulled into the players' parking lot.

After I park my shiny black Porsche, one of two sports cars I own, I head into the arena.

It's eerily quiet in the locker room without all the guys.

I don't like it.

I can't wait till the games start back up. Our holiday break has only been a few days, but it feels way too long.

I'm beyond pumped that we have a game tomorrow night.

Yes!

I am so fucking ready.

As I change into my hockey gear, something strikes me as odd. The person who used to coordinate these events would always come down to the locker room to give me a heads-up on what to expect.

I mean, crap, I still have no fucking clue how things are going to go.

Am I meeting with just one kid at a time for more personalized attention or the whole group at once?

If it is just one kid, what order will they go in?

If it's a group, do I just skate over to them and get started?

What happens then?

Will the kids even be in a group?

Or will they already be skating around out on the ice?

And there's more…

Will there be time for me to sign autographs?

When will that happen exactly?

And when do I present the equipment?

"Shit, that's a lot to think about."

Yet here I stand, dick in hand—well, not literally, but you get the picture—with no fucking guidance.

Who is this rookie coordinator the team hired?

It must be hard to find good help these days.

Ugh!

I'm kind of in a sour mood by the time I hit the ice.

The kids are everywhere—some are skating around and laughing, while others are just standing at center ice, talking.

I'm glad to see that they all seem to be having fun.

It's a good start.

When the large group of kids convened in the middle of the ice begins to part, I get why the new coordinator didn't come to the locker room—"he" is a "she."

And man, this chick is fine.

At least she is from the back.

The new event coordinator has an amazing ass, all taut and tight with the right amount of round. Her glutes look firm and touchable encased in black spandex leggings.

As she remains busy talking with the kids, I continue to check her out.

Damn, even her long blonde ponytail is sexy. I like the way it curls down her lean back, the honey shade contrasting so nicely with the black long-sleeved tech top she has on.

I can't wait to see her face.

To spur her to turn around, I clear my throat rather loudly.

But she pays me no heed.

I guess it's because she's engrossed with a little girl in pigtails.

The other kids in her group are dispersing.

Having heard my throat-clearing, they're now all skating over excitedly.

As one little boy approaches, he exclaims, "It's him! It's him! It's Landen Zehner!"

From there the kids converge on me in a cacophony, like they're all chiming in at once.

"Mr. Zehner, can I have an autograph before we leave today?"

"Can my mom take a picture of us when we get off the ice?"

"When do we start?"

"Can you teach us how to do a slap shot?"

And those are just the questions I catch.

Help!

"Um, er, uh," I blubber. "Ah, why don't you all just go ahead and skate around some more. I'll get all those answers for you in a sec."

The kids comply, heading off in different directions, though they do appear to be a bit confused.

So am I.

This is why I need some damn guidance.

With the throng of children out of the way, I have an unobstructed view of the new event coordinator. She's finishing up with talking to the little girl, who I see now looks like she was crying.

Okay, I'm not so annoyed anymore.

How sweet and thoughtful is it that the new event coordinator is making sure the child is all right?

I like her after all.

I was irritated, but her thoughtfulness with the little girl has touched my heart.

That's why I'm smiling at her before she even turns around.

May as well make a good first impression, right?

And then, almost like she feels my eyes on her, the event coordinator spins to face me.

And just that, my smile falters.

"Holy shit! Cricket?"

Smiling back at me smugly, she skates over.

Now I know why she wanted to wait to confirm our date.

But hold up here one little minute.

This means she knew the entire time last night who the hell I was.

With the realization that I've been played, I narrow my eyes at her as she closes in.

4

WHAT'S WITH THAT LOOK, ZEHNER?

CRICKET

skate up to Landen, picking up speed and spraying him with ice since his green eyes are narrowed at me accusingly.

Ahh, someone doesn't like to be one-upped.

Get used to it, buddy.

I like this game.

And I'm good at playing it.

Casually, I ask, "What's with that look, Zehner?"

"You know," he begins, still clearly seething, "you could've clued me in that you work for the Wolves."

Ooh, he's mad.

This is so much fun.

Good, I'm about to rile him up further.

Shrugging, I reply, "I only started just the other day. Besides…" I snicker. "Where would the fun have been in letting you know I was aware of who you and your teammates were?"

Glaring at me, Landen says tightly, "At least it all makes sense now."

I know where he's going with this, but I play dumb, just…because.

"What makes sense?" I ask, cocking my head.

I'm glad the kids are busy and giving us a wide berth. They must recognize that we're in a heated discussion.

Landen, huffing, grinds out, "It makes sense that you told me to wait till today to decide if I want to go out with you."

Pretending to be bored, I check my pink-painted nails. "Oh, yeah, I forgot about that."

"Sure you did, Cricket."

Uh-oh, he's catching on to my game.

It may be time to end it, seeing as I really do want to go out with him.

Even if he does drives me a little bit nuts with his cockiness.

I drop the playing-it-cool act and flat-out ask, "So what's your answer?"

"Anxious, aren't we?" he retorts, smirking.

Crap, he knows he has me now.

"Er, uh," I sputter.

Shifting on his skates, he snarks, "Just to clarify, I'm asking 'What's the answer to what, Cricket?'"

Using my own tactic against me—jerk!

But Landen is an incredibly hot jerk.

I can't deny that.

He looks amazing standing on the ice in his hockey gear, sans helmet. I'm glad for that, as I'm able to secretly fawn over his messy blond hair, chiseled jaw, and those pretty green eyes.

He's so nice to look at.

Still, I better answer his snotty question before he says something even more obnoxious about me checking him out.

Glancing over at a small group of kids picking out youth hockey sticks that a guy from the ice crew just brought out, I inquire flatly, "Just let me know, Landen, so we can get this event started. Do you want to go out on a date with me or not? It's totally up to you."

I'm certain he's going to say yes, seeing as he's checking me out, just like I was with him a few seconds ago.

He looks happy with what he sees.

Good.

I cough to garner his attention, and his eyes meet mine.

He smiles at me knowingly, saying nothing.

"Hello?" I wave my hand in front of his handsome face. "Did you forget what we're talking about? Hockey players can't be this dumb, can they? Or maybe it's just you."

Swatting my hand away, albeit lightly, he chuckles. "Ha ha ha. You're just full of laughs, aren't you? Did you ever consider maybe I'm still thinking it over?"

I snort. "It takes this much energy?"

Ooh, he doesn't like that.

"You know, Cricket, I'm seriously reconsidering whether I really do want to go out with such a smartass."

Mouth falling open—*this guy!*—I narrow my eyes at him. "Oh, you, you—"

"Yes? Are you upset to hear I may not want to go out with you after all? I bet you are, seeing as you seem pretty damn excited at the prospect of going out with me."

I literally growl at him then. "Grrr…"

He makes me so mad.

Maybe it isn't such a good idea to go out on a date with him.

We may kill each other.

But, damn, he is gorgeous.

"I'm waiting," he says.

Ugh, how did this get turned around onto me?

And with the realization that I'm losing my own game, I give up.

"That's it!" I throw my hands in the air. "You know what? Just forget it. There will be no date. Not now, not ever!"

Huffing loudly, I start to skate far, far away from Landen Zehner.

Too bad I can't skate right off the stupid ice.

5

MIXING SHIT UP

LANDEN

After huffing at me, Cricket skates off.

What a feisty little vixen.

She shouldn't have messed with me, though.

Still, I like this game.

But more than that, I like her.

I'm glad we get to spend the next couple of hours together.

I think she just realized that, by the way.

Smirking, I watch as she abruptly stops at center ice.

Yeah, babe, you still have a job to do...with me.

Slowly, she turns around.

Our eyes meet, and I smile sweetly at her.

See, I can be nice.

And here she comes, skating back over to me, albeit reluctantly.

I suppose that's because I upped her at her own snarky game.

Hey, if she can't stand the heat, she should stay out of the hot kitchen.

Or off the cold ice, as the case may be.

Whatever.

When she reaches me, I can't help but blurt out, "I knew you couldn't stay away from me for too long."

Holding up her hand, she takes a really deep breath. "Just shut up, okay?"

I laugh.

Wow, now she's really glaring at me.

"Aww, don't be mad," I say consolingly. "You still want to hear my answer to your question, right?"

I'm about to say yes, I most definitely want to go out with her. I mean, look at her. She's hot, fun, and she likes to mix it up just like I do.

She really is my kind of girl.

I've just been giving her a hard time, like I did last night.

It's so much fun that I just can't stop myself.

But the truth is I have no qualms about dating a fellow Wolves employee.

It's allowed, but even if it wasn't, I like to live a little dangerously and would probably still go out with her.

Uh, but we may have a problem.

Looks like I pushed it too far with Cricket.

Shaking her head, she says, "No, Landen. Now is not the time to talk about going out on that stupid date. We have a lot of work to do. The kids are our priority here."

She's right, so I capitulate. "Okay. Let's get started."

Cricket is all business from that point on.

Calling the kids over to form a circle around us, she begins organizing them into small groups of three to four.

After she sets the ground rules about everyone taking their turn and being encouraging to one another, she pulls me aside.

"You go ahead and start practicing a few skills drills with the first three groups on this side of the ice. I'll take my groups over to the other side to shoot some pucks into the net. That should keep everyone busy."

I nod. "Okay, sounds good."

Even though I'm trying to be nice and easygoing now, Cricket is choosing to work with her groups as far away from me as possible. I think if she could give them a tour of the upper deck of the arena, it wouldn't put enough distance between us for her liking.

She can't be this mad, though, can she?

I mean, come on, she was giving it to me just as hard.

Speaking of hard, I'd like to give her a few other stiff things.

Well, one in particular.

But alas, we have work to do.

I get started with the first speed drill, which involves skating up and down a section of the ice as fast as we can.

The kids love it!

They're really awesome, so enthusiastic and willing to learn.

That's why when it's time for the next drill—shooting pucks at the net on my side of the ice—I'm more amped than ever.

Unlike Cricket, who's having the kids tap pucks into the net from wherever they are on the ice, I'm going with a more structured approach.

I have my groups line up at different points to shoot the puck from various angles.

It's a great way for me to learn where their strengths and weaknesses lie. It also helps me figure out what we should work on next, which ends up being slap shots.

Most of the kids are pretty amped about that.

And while some of the kids have real, natural talent, others need a little work.

That's why I make sure when it's time for one-on-one sessions, I put in extra effort with the lesser skilled children.

I'm happy to note too that the better ones are following Cricket's advice and being encouraging. They're rooting and cheering on the less talented kids.

Because of that, every single child has a great time.

When our respective drills wrap up, Cricket skates over with her groups so we can switch.

"Is everything going all right?" she asks.

"It's going phenomenally," I reply. "These kids are awesome."

"Right?" She actually smiles at me. "They really are. Oh, and after we're done, we'll surprise them with the equipment."

"Fantastic." I'm feeling truly pumped as I tell her, "I can't wait."

She nods. "They're really going to love that part."

"For sure," I agree.

When the drills are all over, Cricket and I do indeed begin passing out the new equipment.

And the kids are beyond excited.

Seeing them so happy makes me smile.

When I glance over at Cricket, I catch her grinning too.

It's turning into a good day after all.

After all the equipment is passed out, Cricket informs me that there's time for selfies and autographs with the kids and their parents, who are up in the stands.

We have a great time with that too.

Cricket keeps everything super organized and on schedule.

Despite our bickering, I really am impressed with her. The Wolves chose wisely for the event coordinator position.

Once everyone has filed out, amid waves and heartfelt goodbyes, Cricket skates back out onto the ice.

When she starts picking up sticks and pucks that were left lying about, I don't know why, but I head out onto the ice to talk with her.

Skating up to her, I say, "You do know that the ice crew guy usually retrieves all this stuff?"

Skating languorously, three sticks and two pucks in her hand, she shrugs. "Yeah, I know. I just like being out here."

We stop by the bench, where she drops the sticks and pucks over the boards.

When we start skating again, she goes on. "The ice is so relaxing. When I was a kid, my parents signed me up for figure skating lessons. I loved it from day one. Just skating around makes me feel good. Does that make sense?"

Is she kidding?

Chuckling, I reply, "I'm a hockey player, Cricket. Of course that makes sense. To me, the ice is everything."

"Yeah," she mutters, "I guess it would be."

We skate quietly then, along the perimeter of the ice, lost in our own thoughts. I don't know what she's thinking about, but I know what's on my mind—I'm surer than ever that I want to go out with her.

On top of all of her amazing attributes, we share a love of the ice.

She truly is right for me.

Sighing deeply, I finally break the silence. "So about that date…"

Slowing, she glances over at me, quirking a brow. "Yes?"

"I'm not asking you anymore if you want an answer. I'm just going to give it to you."

"Ooh, now we're talking. I like a man who's direct."

"Good. 'Cause I'd like to go out with you. I don't care that we work for the same organization. Is that direct enough for you, Cricket?"

She nods thoughtfully. "Yes, I think it is."

I stop skating, as does she, and then I ask, "So what's your response? Have you changed your mind or do you still plan to back out?"

"Can I?" she asks.

I shrug, though I do feel bad that she may not follow through.

Still, I tell her, "Hey, nothing's set in stone."

"We did make a bet, though," she concedes.

"Yes, we did. And I won."

"You did."

"So what's it going to be?"

She's so quiet that I can't help but prompt, "Do you plan on giving me an answer sometime today?"

"Um…" She cracks a mischievous grin.

"Uh-oh, what's up now?"

Turning to me, she says, "How about if we make my answer dependent on yet another bet?"

I scoff. "Sure. I'm always up for another fun wager."

Smirking triumphantly, she replies, "Cool, so am I. So here's the bet—if you can catch me, Landen, *then* I'll go out with you. In fact, I'll go anywhere you want me to go."

Faster than I ever would've expected, she suddenly takes off.

But faster than I'm sure *she* ever expected, I chase after her.

6

HEDGING MY BET

CRICKET

D o I want Landen to lose?

Hell no!

That's why I hedged my bet.

I mean, come on. Like there's any chance on this planet he can't catch me.

I think not.

Landen is one of the fastest hockey players in the league, for fuck's sake.

So yeah, he's going to win.

Doesn't mean I can't give it my all, though, right?

Fast as I can, pumping my arms and legs like a madwoman, I zip up the ice.

I have a good head start, but before I even come close to reaching the other side, Landen is on me.

Mmm, I feel his warm body closing in.

I like that.

I actually slow down on purpose so he can capture me.

But that only serves to throw him off.

He's skating at such a high rate of speed that when he wraps his arms around my waist, spinning me to face him, we almost career into the boards.

"Ahhh," I cry out.

"Don't worry." He pulls me in more securely, spinning us around so he can take the brunt. "I got you, babe."

He does.

Landen's reflexes are amazing.

Creating a huge spray of ice with his skates as he lifts me up, he stops on a dime before we ever make contact with the wooden boards.

"Whoa, that was close," I breathe out.

His hands remain on either side of my waist as he lowers me down to the ice.

My skates touch and, placing my own hands on his wide chest, the Wolves black-and-red emblem on the front of his jersey so smooth and silky beneath my palms, I steady myself.

It's not just my skates that have me off-balance.

It's Landen.

"That *was* close," he replies. "But we're okay."

"We are," I agree, "thanks to your quick actions."

He leans back against the boards, and it dawns on me then just how truly ready he was to take the hit if we had crashed.

That melts me even further, like literally.

I press into him, and he inhales sharply.

When I look up, our eyes meet.

His sage greens are piercing up close like this, and I can't help but murmur, "Wow."

"Yeah, wow," he replies, meaning something else entirely, I'm sure.

I should back away, but I can't.

Clearing my throat, I mumble, "You, uh, were great with the kids today."

"As were you," he replies quietly.

I shrug, and he moves his hands around to my back, where he starts caressing slowly.

Oh my God, that feels so good.

I'm tingly all over, and my heart skips a beat.

All I want right now is to kiss Landen Zehner.

I think he wants that too.

As my gaze travels to his lips, I see that he's smiling.

But then it becomes too much.

I suddenly feel unsure and start stammering, "We, uh… We should get off the ice, yeah?"

"Why?" He raises a brow. "There's no one around."

I sputter, "Uh, but the guy from the ice crew could come back at any time."

"Eh." Landen shrugs. "He could, but he's not here right now."

I can't argue with that. "No, no he's not."

"So what do you want, Cricket?"

Landen's voice is so smooth, so seductive.

Fuck it.

I'm done fighting what we both so clearly desire.

I blurt out, "I want you to kiss me."

"Finally," Landen growls, "a straight answer."

"Yes, finally."

With no hesitation at all, his lips crash down onto mine.

7

SUBLIME

LANDEN

Kissing Cricket is sublime. Her lips are full and sweet, and I can't get enough.

Delicious...

This is an amazing communion of mouths—lips interlocked, tongues touching, and just breathing each other in.

It is perfect.

When we stop for air, I shift and murmur into her ear, "I want you so much right now."

Cricket slumps against me and groans, "Unh, Landen, don't say that. You're killing me here."

"No, sweetheart..." I trail soft kisses down her neck slowly. "It's you who's killing me. But...in...the...best...way...possible."

She lets out a little sigh, and we basically attack each other.

Who cares that we're still on the ice?

Not me, not her.

No, her hands wind into my hair, and I slide mine down to cup her ass, squeezing her firm cheeks.

She gasps.

And I groan.

Then, out of nowhere, someone clears their throat.

Shit.

We break apart, both of us slumping against the boards.

We pretend as if nothing is happening here, as if we weren't just all over each other.

And then we see that the throat-clearer is the guy from the ice crew.

Yeah, we weren't just dry-humping each other on the ice, dude.

I don't think he'll believe that.

Still, Cricket clears her throat and says very loudly, "So, yes, Mr. Zehner, that concludes our event for today. Thank you for staying to impart your, uhhh, input. It was quite helpful."

The ice crew guy, who's really just a kid of about nineteen, starts laughing.

Even I can't keep a straight face.

"I think we've been busted," I whisper to Cricket.

"Yeah." She sighs. "It would seem so."

The ice crew guy, shaking his head, skates out onto the ice and starts retrieving the sticks and pucks Cricket never got to.

As he approaches us, he says, "Don't worry. I didn't see a thing."

Since he so clearly did see quite a lot, but is being cool about it, I tell him, "Hey, thanks, man. It's much appreciated."

Even though there are no explicit rules regarding Wolves employees dating, Cricket did just start her job a few days ago. I don't think public displays of affection between us, especially on my work surface, would be appreciated.

So yeah, no, discretion is the way to go.

I'm glad the kid's on board.

Looking at me, Cricket says, "I guess we should get off the ice, huh?"

I nod. "Yeah, I think so."

As we begin skating over to one of the exits along the boards, I say, "So, about that date…"

Cricket, snickering, raises a brow. "Yes?"

No more messing around. I get right to the point. "When do you want to go out? I have a game tomorrow, which I'm sure you know. But I'm free the next night."

Winking over at me, she says, "As luck would have it, Landen, so am I."

I guess she's done playing games too.

Our impromptu make-out session seems to have sealed the deal.

We're both dying to go out and continue this fun.

"Good." I nod. "We'll go out Friday night, then."

"Friday it is," she says cheerfully.

"Perfect."

We reach the exit, and I flip the latch to swing open the wood door for her.

After she carefully steps off the ice, blonde ponytail bouncing, I follow.

"Is seven a good time to pick you up?" I ask from behind her. "We can go to dinner, then do whatever you want. A movie, dancing—"

"I have an idea actually," Cricket interrupts, spinning to face me.

"What?" I practically crash into her but, of course, don't. "You don't like dinner?"

She laughs. "No, no, the dinner part sounds great. But afterward, how do you feel about us hitting up the casino and playing a little blackjack?" Giving me a stern look, she adds, "As I recall, I have some money to win back."

Man, I am falling for this woman already.

Folding my arms across my chest, I retort, "I think you mean you have some more money to *lose*...to me."

"Ha, you wish, Landen."

I raise a brow. "Wanna bet?"

Placing her hands on her waist, and looking super cute, she says, "Are we talking about another side wager here?"

I shrug. "Yeah, why not? Winner chooses whatever they want. And like before, it has to be a surprise."

She pretends to mull it over, but I know she'll take the bet.

She's a gambler like me.

Sure enough, with a flip of her ponytail as she turns her back on me, she says over her shoulder, "You're on, Zehner."

8

THE BEST PERK

CRICKET

The really cool thing about working for the Wolves is I get to go to the games for free. I was excited when I first heard about this perk, but now that I'm getting to know Landen, I'm beyond pumped.

It should come as no surprise, then, that once I'm finishing up at the office the day after the event with Landen and the kids, my boss, Ahren, hands me a ticket for tonight's game against the Kings and I almost grab her up in a huge hug.

Of course, I do no such thing.

But I do tell her, "Thank you."

When I check the seat assignment on the ticket and see where I'll be, my enthusiasm ramps up even higher.

"Holy crap! I'm behind the Wolves' bench? I can't believe this. This is the best, Ahren. You are the greatest boss in the world."

Smiling, she says, "Just go and have fun, Cricket."

"Don't worry," I assure her. "I will."

When she sighs, though, I have to ask, "Wait. What's wrong?"

Swishing her hand through the air, she says, "Oh, it's nothing bad. I just feel crappy I could only secure one ticket for you. It's just that it was such short notice with you being a new hire and all. Anyway, from here on out, I should be able to get you two tickets most game nights. This is the first game back after the break, however, and it seemed everyone and their brother wanted a ticket."

"I understand," I say.

And I do.

Still, Ahren assures me, "Next time, I promise, definitely plan to bring a friend."

"That'd be great." I smile at her. "I will."

I instantly think of Bettina, my grad school friend who moonlights at the casino. She loves hockey almost as much as I do, so yeah, she's definitely the one I'll call when I have that extra ticket.

For tonight, though, I'm on my own.

That's fine. I can sit and drool over Landen as much as I want. With no one to chat with, he'll be my sole focus.

Oh, and the game will be on my radar as well.

Just not as much as Landen will be.

Hee hee.

Since I'll be seated behind the players' bench, Landen will have as much of a clear view of me as I will of him.

That's why later that afternoon, after work and once I'm home, I decide to go all out and dress as cutely as possible.

Skinny dark-wash jeans, black leather ankle boots with heels to die for, and a black-and-red Wolves jersey over a long-sleeved white tee and I'm good to go.

Before I leave my bedroom to hit the road, I pull my hair up into a high ponytail.

But then I hesitate and let it tumble back down.

I take some extra time to curl the ends for a little more bounce.

Now I'm ready to go.

Unfortunately, since I lost a little time messing with my hair, once I'm parked—thank goodness for the almost-empty employee lot—I head into the arena and discover it's packed and rocking.

That's fine.

The excitement is palpable, and I'm quickly swept up in the emotion.

When I reach my section, a helpful usher assists me in finding my seat behind the Wolves' bench.

It's like freaking right in the center!

Smiling like crazy, I settle in.

The guys aren't out yet. They're still in the locker room getting ready for the game.

But warm-ups are coming up.

According to the countdown clock up on the big Jumbotron hanging from the rafters, the players should be out in about four minutes and ten seconds.

Make that nine, eight…

I tap my booted foot in time with the countdown and the upbeat music that's playing. The game hasn't even started and I'm already caught up in the fun atmosphere.

I don't even care that I'm alone.

As the time ticks down, the volume in the arena increases.

And then a horn sounds, and the players from both teams fly out onto the ice.

Almost everyone jumps up out of their seats, including me.

The Kings are booed, and the Wolves are bombarded with screams and cheers.

I even find myself whooping and hollering.

The guys all skate so damn fast that they're like a blur out on the ice.

No wonder Landen caught me with such ease.

He probably wasn't even trying.

My mind goes to what occurred *after* he caught me, and we were up against the boards.

That makes me smile and blush at the same time.

Biting my lip, I peer over to the exact same spot where our heated make-out session occurred, against a board with an ad for a local pizza joint.

That's when I see Landen.

Be still my heart!

Wow, I already like this guy so much.

Maybe too much.

Landen is stopped next to our board. He's leaning on his stick, talking with one of the other players while he waits for his turn to shoot pucks at their goalie who just got in place in the net.

I squint to see who he's chatting with.

It's Blake Cavaletti.

Blake is a right winger and plays on the third line with Landen. They're good friends, having both been traded from New York City teams this past summer.

I heard Blake got married recently to another player's sister. I think her name is Noelle. I know for sure that her brother is Noel Sandlund.

Hmm, looks like all my research on the players is paying off.

I feel like I know some of them already.

If nothing else, I certainly know a lot about them.

But I want to know more, especially about Landen.

I'm going to have so many questions on our date tomorrow night.

He better be ready for me.

Yeah, in more ways than one, I think as I lick my lips.

Landen, almost like he can feel my eyes on him, glances over at me.

I'm still standing, so I wave.

He nods in acknowledgment.

We hold each other's gazes then.

Even from halfway across the arena, the energy between us stirs to life.

Blake is still talking to Landen, but he's not paying a bit of attention.

He's looking at me, smiling.

I smile back.

Finally, Blake looks over to see what's captured Landen's attention.

Chuckling and shaking his head, he turns back around and taps his friend with his stick.

He then skates over to the front of the net to take his practice shots.

Blake gets three pucks in, but the goaltender stops two.

Landen is up next.

He pops in four of what will be five practice shots in quick succession.

"Wow," I murmur. "Color me impressed."

He has only one puck left to shoot.

Glancing up at me, he mouths, "This one's for you."

Winding up, his eyes still on me and clearly throwing off his goaltender, he wails the puck into the net.

Now I'm more than impressed.

I am in full and total lust for Landen Zehner.

THIS ONE'S FOR CRICKET

LANDEN

am on fire.

Four shots, and all of them whizz past our goaltender.

It's only a warm-up, but after I shoot the final puck into the net for Cricket, I decide to devote my whole performance on the ice tonight to her.

Talk about a motivator.

And is it ever!

Early in the first period, Blake sets me up with a beautiful pass while I'm out in front of the Kings' net, battling with one of their defensemen.

The guy is trying to get me out of the crease but ends up backing me into the perfect position to score.

Winding up, I whiz the puck past the goaltender the dumbass

defenseman is unintentionally screening.

Score!

"Thanks, you stupid fucker," I murmur to the defenseman as I skate away to celebrate with Blake and my other teammates.

The dude does not like that.

Skating up from behind, the fucker cross-checks me.

I spin around to face him, ready to roll.

But then I decide not to retaliate.

The referee has already seen what the defenseman did, and he's now watching for my reaction.

Why get sent to the penalty box, right?

So I just stand casually, smirking at the jerk defenseman as he gets called for the cross-checking penalty.

Good, serves you right.

It's all upside for our team from there.

Our captain, Brent Oliver, scores a goal right before the second period ends.

And then I pick up an assist on a Blake Cavaletti goal midway through the third.

We end up winning the game.

I start thinking that maybe I need to dedicate *all* my games to Cricket.

Yeah, maybe I should.

At dinner the next night, while Cricket and I are out on our first date, I share with her that I dedicated the game to her.

And then I tell her, "It ended up being one of my best of the season."

Taking a sip of merlot, I set the glass back down and add, "All because of you, pretty lady."

"Oh, Landen, stop," she purrs demurely.

"It's true," I insist.

Jesus, she's blushing, and it's so adorable.

Waving her hand dismissively, Cricket states quietly, "I'm sure you would've scored those points no matter what."

"No." I swipe my mouth with my cloth napkin, having just indulged in a juicy bite of filet mignon. "I don't think so. I felt extra motivated playing for you."

"That's sweet of you to say," Cricket replies softly as she toys with the stem of her wineglass, the merlot swishing.

She looks beautiful tonight.

I've thought that from the start.

I've been enthralled with her since I picked her up for our date.

Yeah, the moment she opened the door of her townhouse, I had no choice but to stop and drink her in. From her beautiful, flowing honey-blonde hair down to her sparkly, shimmering silver dress and black stiletto heels, I was a goner.

"Wow" was all I could say.

Good thing she seemed just as enamored with me.

That made me glad I chose to wear my sharpest black suit tonight.

It's cool too that we sort of match.

We didn't plan our monochromatic attire. It's just the way things worked out.

The only splash of color for me is my siren red tie, and she has tiny red bows on the backs of her heels.

We look good together.

Like a couple.

Yeah, just like that.

Taking a small sip of wine and setting her glass down, Cricket asks, "What are you smiling about over there, Landen?"

Shit, I can't tell her what I was just thinking.

It's far too soon for a we-make-a-good-couple talk.

So I go with something that's also true, but a little less incriminating. "I, uh, I was just thinking about what a nice night we're having. That's all."

"I'm having a great time too. The steak is excellent." She pauses, peering over at me meaningfully. "But the company is even better."

Nodding in agreement, I tell her, "I'll drink to that."

We raise our wineglasses and tap the rims.

Cricket is about to say something more, but the waitress shows up to clear our plates.

Damn interruption.

She asks if we'd like dessert, but Cricket and I say no and just ask for espressos.

The waitress, jotting that down on her order pad, murmurs, "Certainly, Mr. Zehner."

"Hmm, so she does know who you are," Cricket says once the server is out of sight. "And she was playing it so cool up until now."

"She was." I shrug. "But it happens."

"Clearly," Cricket says, smiling and shaking her head. "And look at you, just so calm and cool about it."

"It's just part of the job," I assure her.

The waitress returns with our espressos, and after she leaves, I lean back in my chair.

"So, Cricket," I begin, "how about if you tell me a little more about you. Do you realize I don't even know your last name yet?"

Her eyes widen. "Holy crap, you're right. It's Nance."

"Ah, got it. So where are you from originally, Miss Nance? I feel like no one I meet is ever actually from Las Vegas."

"I'm not," she replies. "I was born and raised in Phoenix. I came up here for school. What about you? Do you hail from the East Coast or the West Coast, or somewhere in the middle?"

Chuckling, I tell her, "I'm from the east, though not anywhere close to the actual coast. I'm from a little town called Rose. It's in upstate Michigan."

Nodding, she muses, "Huh, I've never heard of it."

"Not many people have."

Folding her hands on the table, she leans forward. "Okay, next question. Do you have any siblings?"

I nod. "Yes, I have two older brothers. What about you?"

"I have a sister. She's nineteen."

"That's cool."

"Oooh, I just thought of another question." Cricket props her elbows up on the table, placing her chin in one palm. "How'd you get so good at blackjack?"

I snort. "You're one to talk. You're like a damn card shark. I should be the one asking you that question."

"Sure. But you go first."

"All right." I take a sip of espresso. "I learned how to play cards with the guys on the team plane. We have a lot of long flights to get to some of the games, and cards are a way to pass the time. You end up picking up some tips and tricks after a while."

Leaning back in her seat, she says, "I see. That makes sense."

"So where did you learn how to play?" I inquire. "Card school?"

That makes her laugh. "Ha ha. No, no card school for me. I actually learned how to play online."

We look at each other, and I can't help but burst out laughing.

"What?" Cricket says. "It's true."

Still chuckling, I say, "It's just that you're so good. I would not have expected an online card school to produce such talent."

Preening, she replies, "Why, thank you, Landen. I think I may just be a natural, though."

I shrug and concede, "Maybe so."

Turning playful, she replies, "There are no 'maybes' about it, mister. That's why I know I'm going to kick your butt later tonight when we get to the casino."

She levels me with her stunning azure eyes, and I suddenly have an epiphany—I don't really want to sit in a stuffy casino back room with her and a bunch of strangers. I have a better idea, one where we can be alone.

So slowly, I say, "Ah, yes, our little wager. About that… I'm thinking maybe we should change our plans."

Brow creasing, she asks, "Change our plans? How do you mean?"

"Eh…" I shrug. "Do you really feel like playing cards in a back room tonight with a bunch of people we don't know? Or would you rather do something that's sure to get your heart rate racing? Something with just us. And don't worry, there can still be a bet involved."

"Hmm, I have to say I am intrigued." Cricket crosses her arms, and she really does look interested. "But you're going to have to be more specific before I commit. What exactly do you have in mind, Mr. Zehner?"

10

MY HEART IS DEFINITELY RACING

CRICKET

Landen suggests a change in plans, and I let him know that I'm open to that.

Hey, what can I say?

I like mixing it up.

And I actually don't feel like sitting in the back room of a casino with strangers.

I'm up for something more one-on-one with Landen.

Truth be told, I'd like to get *really* one-on-one with him.

With a naughty smirk, so maybe he'll see where my thoughts are heading, I ask what he has in mind.

Smiling and shaking his head—I think he knows—he tells me, "We'll get to that, Miss Nance. But first…"

"Yes?"

I flutter my lashes, and he mumbles, "Woman, you are killing me here."

Folding my hands on the table like a good girl, I promise, "Okay, I'll behave. Go ahead and tell me your idea."

Muttering something about me hopefully not behaving later, he then says, "You may have noticed the car I picked you up in tonight."

I snort. "Yeah, it would've been hard not to notice. It's a freaking Ferrari in, like, fire-engine red."

"That would be the one," he says smugly.

"So…" I unfold my hands and lean forward. "What does your flashy car have to do with our change in plans?"

Smirking, Landen says, "Well, if you know anything about that flashy car, you know it goes really fast. Like *really* fucking fast."

I'm curious as to where this is heading, so I prompt, "Go on."

Sighing, he shares, "I was never really able to open up the Ferrari back in New York. It was just too congested. Even the back roads outside of the city were packed with cars almost all the time. And even when they weren't, they were always patrolled."

"I'd imagine," I interject.

"But out here in Nevada…" Landen gives me a wink. "It's a different story. I've found plenty of lonely, quiet stretches of road in the untamed parts of the desert. No police, no anybody. In fact, I discovered a particularly cool area just recently."

"Yeah? How'd you come upon that?"

Shrugging, he says, "I was out driving around aimlessly one night just for something to do, and I found a road way out in the middle of nowhere that was completely desolate. I mean, not a soul to be found. I've gone out there a few times since, and no one is ever there. It's this really long stretch of paved road that goes on for miles. I think it's a part of a highway that was never finished. Anyway, I'm sure there are cars that travel it from time to time, as it's not closed off, but I think no one is out there much, if ever, late at night. "

"Oooh, I like where this is going," I confess.

And I do.

This would definitely mean more one-on-one time with Landen.

Maybe he'll even kiss me again.

If this place he's speaking of is so desolate, there would surely be no interruptions.

Landen appears pleased that I'm into his change of plans.

"I knew you were my kind of girl," he states quietly.

My cheeks warm.

I hope I'm not blushing again.

I know I was earlier when he told me he dedicated the game to me and it made him play better.

Even if it does embarrass me, I love that Landen just freaking says what's on his mind.

It's refreshing.

"So," he continues, "what I'm suggesting is that we take the Ferrari out to that isolated part of the desert and get a little wild on the road. What do you say?"

"I say hell yeah!"

Landen starts smiling like crazy.

And what a smile it is.

It makes me want to give him more reasons to smile like that.

I can think of a few that might accomplish it.

Clearing my throat, I look away.

Better not get too far ahead of myself.

It's just that Landen makes me want to cut loose.

He brings out *my* wild side.

I want to show him that aspect of me in more ways too, like in bed.

Phew, it's getting hot in here.

Good thing he's distracted, flagging down the waitress and asking for the check.

My lusty thoughts will remain undetected.

After Landen pays for dinner, we retrieve his car from the valet and head out to the deep, dark desert.

When I look through the windshield, I see there's a big full moon up in the sky. It's huge and orange, and there are a billion stars around it, twinkling brightly.

There's definitely something romantic about this scene.

And my heart is racing already.

It pretty much stays the same way as we leave the bright city lights behind and travel to the back roads where the population becomes sparser and sparser.

Soon it'll be just Landen and me, the sports car, and this serene desert.

I love it.

When we reach what I assume is our destination—a long, perfectly straight stretch of paved road in the middle of nowhere—I'm more amped than ever that we changed our plans.

This night is amazing already.

Dinner was great, conversation was fantastic, and now I'm spending alone time with Landen as we're about to open up the Ferrari on a dark, lonely road.

I can only imagine what may come next.

His lips felt so good on mine out there on the ice.

He felt so good.

I can't quit thinking about that kiss.

I need more.

As I sigh longingly, Landen, having just pulled off to the side of the road, asks, "What are you thinking about over there? You've been really quiet since we left the restaurant. You're not having second thoughts, are you?"

Is he kidding?

"No way!" I exclaim. "Not even close."

"Good." Slipping off his suit jacket, which takes a little work in the tight quarters, he then loosens his red tie and undoes the first two buttons of his shirt. "Though feel free to share what you *are* thinking about, pretty lady."

Er, um, I don't think so.

And now my thoughts are dirtier than ever having just watched him ditch his jacket and get more comfortable.

I'd like to help him out of that dress shirt completely. His muscles look so big and defined beneath the crisp white cotton.

I don't say any of that, though.

But I do share part of where my mind is when I tell him, "I'm just thinking that I can't wait to see what this car can do."

He nods approvingly. "That's the spirit. And trust me, Cricket, this car can do a lot."

I believe him.

Even as we're sitting here idling, I can totally hear and feel the power of the engine.

Tapping the steering wheel, Landen asks, "Would you like to go first?"

"Wait, what?" I stare over at him incredulously. "You're going to let me drive your car?"

"Well, yeah." He laughs. "That's the whole idea. It wouldn't be too much fun for you to just sit over there in the passenger seat while I go wild. The thrill is in driving this car, Cricket."

I cringe. "Um, but what if I wreck it?"

"You won't."

"How do you know that?"

He motions to the open road. "Look out there. This stretch here is long and straight. And, as you can see, there are no other cars. Nothing. It's just you and me and"—he pats the dash—"this fine piece of automotive machinery, raring to go."

I quickly acquiesce. "Okay, you convinced me. I mean, how can I argue with that kind of reasoning?"

"You can't." Peering over at me, he asks again, "So, should I go first, or do you want to have the honor?"

Landen is so confident in me and my driving abilities. It's quite trusting of him to allow me to drive his expensive car.

And that just proves to me even more that he really is an amazing guy.

Breathing in deeply, and then exhaling slowly, I say, "I'll go first."

"Excellent. You're going to have a blast." Landen pops open his door. "Let's switch places."

"Yeah." I snicker nervously. "I guess that would help."

Yeesh, if I thought my heart was beating uncontrollably earlier...

But once I find myself behind the wheel, my nervousness starts to dissipate.

In fact, I begin to feel incredibly empowered.

"I can see why you like this car," I say, adjusting the seat and the rearview mirror.

"Right?" As I'm reaching down and slipping my stiletto heels off,

Landen adds softly, "You look really good over there, by the way."

"I *feel* really good over here," I tell him, tossing my pumps into the back.

I do feel amazing.

I feel so good, in fact, that I come up with an idea for another wager.

Hey, he did say we could still bet on something, right?

Well, I have a good one.

I'm not telling Landen, but if I win, I'm going to insist he take me to his bed tonight, no delays.

I'm not saying that we have to fuck each other's brains out—not yet, anyway—but I want to experience him in some kind of a sexual way.

I think he'll be cool with that.

Nah, I'm sure he will.

He is a man, after all.

So let's get this out on the table, Cricket.

Smiling slyly, I say, "Before we begin, let's make another bet."

Landen laughs. "Shit, you know I'm up for anything you have in mind."

I quickly qualify, "It has to be another wager where neither of us shows their hand, meaning we only tell what we want once one of us wins."

"Sure. That works for me. So what's the bet?"

Putting my foot on the clutch and the car in first gear, I say, "It's easy and straightforward. Whoever hits the fastest speed out here wins."

With that on the table, I peel out.

MY KIND OF CRAZY

LANDEN

The Ferrari takes off into the darkness, and Cricket and I are slammed back into our seats by the sheer g-force.

Shit, this woman is crazy.

But she's my kind of crazy.

I wonder what she's going to ask for if she wins.

I know what I want—I want her to be my girl.

What I mean by that is I want for there to be no other guys in her life.

I want a chance to woo her properly without competition.

Not that I don't think I'd pull ahead of any guy she'd potentially date. I just want her for myself and undistracted by another man.

But first I have to win.

And I don't know that I will.

Cricket is fearless.

We're flying.

It's like we're in a tunnel traveling at warp speed.

Everything is a blur, the dark desert endless.

I glance over at the speedometer.

We're going eighty, ninety, ninety-five...

But right before we hit one hundred miles per hour, Cricket eases up on the gas.

We stay at ninety-nine, then drop down to ninety-eight, ninety-seven...

I start smiling.

Now I know for sure that I am going to win.

Slowing down to a steady thirty-five, Cricket exclaims, "Wow! That was exhilarating. I think I hit ninety-nine."

I confirm, "That sounds about right."

Slowing down even more and then easing off to the side of the road, the gravel on the berm crunching beneath the tires, Cricket stops and pulls up on the emergency brake, leaving the car idling in neutral.

"You're next," she says, reaching to the back to retrieve her heels.

She's so damn confident. She thinks she's got this thing sewn up, like I'm afraid to top one hundred.

Ha!

I let her gloat, though.

"All right." I open the passenger door, smiling to myself. "My turn."

"I can't wait to see how you do," Cricket says, still humming with excitement. "That was so much fun, Landen."

"You did really well," I tell her as I start to get out of the car. "You were fearless."

Before I can exit, though, she catches my arm.

I look over to see her raising a perfectly arched brow. "Thanks, but did I do well enough to win?"

I shrug. "I guess we'll see."

Before she can ask for elaboration, I hop out.

Cricket gets out of the car as well, and as we pass in the back, she gives me a high-five. "Good luck," she says, "but not too much."

That makes me chuckle.

She doesn't know what she's in for.

Ninety-nine mph is just getting started for me.

I show her that when, a few minutes later, I'm the one accelerating down the dark road.

Pressed back into our seats once more, I inch the speedometer up above one hundred.

Cricket gasps out, "Holy crap, dude, you are so wild."

Ha, if she only knew.

This is just the tip of the iceberg.

Since she doesn't sound scared, just wound up, I press the gas pedal down a little more.

We hit one-ten, then one-twenty.

But even I have my limits.

I'm wild, but I don't have a death wish for either of us.

I ease up on the gas, slowing down considerably.

Cricket blows out a breath. "Yeesh, I think you won, Landen. You definitely surpassed my ninety-nine."

"I did," I agree, glancing over at her as we slow to a steady and super-safe twenty-five. "Were you scared?"

Before she can answer, I pull off to the side of the road.

While we sit idling, she blows out a breath.

"No," she says at last, "I wasn't scared. Not really. Maybe a little nervous, but I knew I was in good hands."

"You were," I assure her. "And you always will be. I always have control, and I'd never put you in any real danger. I mean, sure, driving that fast, there's always a risk something could go wrong. But I wouldn't be unnecessarily reckless."

"I know." Cricket peers down at her lap. "Like I said, I feel safe with you."

Chuckling, I ask, "Even when we were going a hundred and twenty miles per hour?"

She looks over at me, and, God, those eyes. They're stunning even in the soft glow of the amber dashboard lights.

I swear, from this day forward, I will forever remember her eyes and the shimmery sparkle of her silver dress in the orange moon glow.

Softly, she says, "Yes, Landen, even then."

I want so much to lean over and kiss her, out here in the dark desert under the big full moon.

But before I have the chance to do that, she asks, "So what do you want? You won the bet, so it's your choice."

I raise a brow. "Do I get to choose anything at all?"

She shrugs, her dress shimmering even more. "Yes, I guess so. We didn't state that there'd be stipulations."

I warn, "You know this could be dangerous, right?"

Smiling over at me, she says, "I know. But I told you that I trust you."

Man, I think she really does.

That makes it real easy for me to then say, "Then be exclusive with me. Don't go out with anyone else, okay? Give me a real chance, and let's see where this can go."

Cricket is staring at me now, her big azure eyes wide. "Wow. You don't just drive fast, you move fast too. This is only our first date, you know?"

"I know." I shrug. "But what can I say? Maybe I just know when something feels right."

"And you think this is right? You think *we* are right for each other?"

I admit, "I do, Cricket. I really do."

She shakes her head. "Man, I don't know. This is a lot to take in."

"Not really. And remember"—I wink over at her—"I did win the bet."

"Yes, you did." She bites her lip, contemplating for a minute or so. At last, she says, "Okay, let's give it a try. I agree to date you exclusively."

I knew she'd give in.

Or at least, I hoped she would.

"See," I tease, "that wasn't so hard."

"No, it wasn't." She smiles at me. "I feel good about this—*us*—too."

Reaching over, I cup her cheek. "You won't regret it, Cricket. I promise."

"You sound so confident," she murmurs.

"I am."

"And why's that?"

Leaning in, I press my lips to hers and tell her, "Because I am going to treat you so fucking well you won't ever even *think* about another guy."

12

SWEET RELEASE

CRICKET

Hmm, that's a tall order.

Landen just told me he's going to treat me "so fucking well" that I won't ever even think about another guy.

Well, so far, he's right.

His mouth feels so good against mine, and his kisses are amazing.

The best part is that this time, there's no one around to interrupt us.

I can't believe he wants me to date him exclusively.

I can get into that, though.

I think I just did.

Mmm, yes.

His excellent kisses continue.

Still, a little part of me is worried.

I like Landen. I like him a lot.

But are we moving too fast, declaring exclusivity after only one date?

Is this crazy?

It probably is, but I don't care.

Not right now.

This right here—his lips on mine, his hands winding in my hair, tugging desperately—feels too damn good to regret anything.

Tilting his head, Landen captures my mouth from a different angle.

Everything about him is perfection, from his rock-hard body to his tender and soft touches.

He is a dichotomy that makes me want him so much more.

And I mean right the hell now.

We're going to be exclusive, right?

Why not just go for it?

Groaning and gasping, I crawl up onto my knees in the passenger seat.

My goal is to climb over onto Landen's lap, but I can't.

It's not my dress that's in the way—the shimmery ruched fabric has enough stretch. It's the stupid tight quarters of the Ferrari that's affording me very little maneuvering room.

Breaking apart, I state breathlessly, "Okay, this car is awesome and all, but it's clearly not made for this."

I motion to our bodies, and that makes Landen laugh.

"Here," he says. "Hold up a sec." Sliding his seat back as far as possible, he hits a lever that raises the steering wheel up and out of the way. "Come on over now." He pats his lap invitingly.

Even though there's barely any illumination and his pants are dark, I can tell he's aroused.

I want that.

Hiking my dress up high enough to flash him my panties, and making him catch his breath, I climb over the console and straddle him.

"What now?" I ask.

"This," he growls, his mouth covering mine.

It's like we can't get enough of each other.

I breathe him in, tasting him, my hands clutching at his wide chest, tangling in his silky dark blond hair, and then finally reaching down and grasping his rigid length.

Yes!

As I stroke him through his pants, Landen's hands do wonderful things—rounding over the curve of my ass, lifting me up, trailing his fingers along my inner thigh.

I undo his belt and unzip his pants, gasping, "I need your hand a little higher."

I know we can't do all that much in the car, no matter how far back the seat goes, but my body is crying for some kind of sweet relief.

As is his, based on how fucking hard he is.

I slip my hand into his boxer briefs and realize it looks like I'll be collecting on this bet after all, even though I didn't win. I wanted something sexual to happen, and here we are.

Landen's fingers begin to inch closer and closer to where I want and need him so badly.

But he's moving oh so slowly.

"Tease," I moan.

He stops for a second, pretending to be aghast. "Me, a tease? Never."

I growl, "Then touch me for real, damn it."

He does.

And holy hell!

The man knows what he's doing—making me so hot I'm about to explode.

It's a slow burn, a torturous building.

And I love it.

Leaning my forehead against his shoulder, I gasp and continue to stroke his impressive length.

When he skims over my soaked panties, I swallow hard.

Softly, he coos, "Ahh, you're so wet for me, beautiful. I feel your heat."

"You do this to me," I murmur.

"Yes, I do."

He's so smug.

But he has every right to be, as he already has me so close to the brink.

"Please, Landen," I cry out.

"Please what?"

"Don't keep me waiting. I want more."

While he pumps his cock into my hand, his fingers slide beneath the silky material of my panties and he begins to finally, and skillfully, work my clit.

Holy fuck, does Landen know what he's doing.

As I stroke him harder and harder, he strums me like an instrument he's been playing all of his life.

"I'm so close, Landen," I tell him. "*So* close."

"Come for me, baby. Let's come together."

"Yes."

Just as I feel him shuddering and climaxing into my hand, his thumb working my clit along with two fingers pumping into me, I also fall apart.

"Landen," I sigh as I collapse against him, burying my head in his shoulder once more.

I can't move.

I can't speak.

I'm in total bliss.

I'm glad Landen's more cognizant.

He reaches into the map holder at the base of the door and grabs a handful of napkins.

"Good thing I stopped for fast food the other day," he says as he cleans us both up.

"Yeah, good thing. You're so good to me," I reply softly.

He whispers back, "I promised you I would be, right?"

"Yes, yes you did."

"And just think," he goes on, "this is only the beginning."

13

THE SOUND OF PAINTING

LANDEN

Over the next several weeks, in between games and Cricket working team events, we spend pretty much all of our free time together.

It's been quick, but we're officially dating one another.

And, as I requested, there are no other men for her.

No additional women for me, either.

It's only fair, and what we ended up mutually deciding the day after I won the driving bet.

It's working out great.

I have no regrets about rushing into things so quickly, nor does Cricket.

She's told me as much.

Interestingly enough, though, the one thing we've held off on is moving forward physically.

This is like a complete reversal for me. I've always been a "love 'em and leave 'em" kind of a guy.

But Cricket makes me want to be different.

She has from the start.

I've enjoyed this moving slowly in the physical area, as it's allowed me to explore my feelings for her.

And they are intense.

That's exactly why I'm going to need her under me soon.

I can't wait forever, nor can she.

I mean, we still mess around a lot—hell, do we ever!—but I've yet to fuck her. And there's no reason for us not to go there. We've had all the necessary talks about birth control and diseases, and we're both clean. She even went to get the Depo shot a couple of weeks ago.

You know, for when it does happen.

I guess now we're just waiting for the right time.

Maybe it'll be today?

Or tomorrow?

Even next week.

I don't know.

I just know it'll be soon.

There's something in the air—tension, anticipation.

Yeah, I think we know it's about to happen real soon.

Cricket is coming over today to help me paint a spare bedroom I'm turning into a home office. The room is currently a very drab pale yellow color. And I fucking hate yellow, especially that crap shade.

I've decided to go with a nice teal that will match the dark teakwood furniture—desk, file cabinet, and credenza—I recently ordered.

I check the time.

It's two o'clock.

Cricket should be here any minute.

Good thing I'm almost ready, having just changed into old gray sweats and a ratty white tee, clothes suitable for painting.

As I head out of my bedroom to the big spiral staircase that leads downstairs, I hear Cricket coming in through the front door.

Yeah, I gave her a key the other day so she can let herself in whenever she comes over.

She did the same for me, as we're always at either my place or hers.

The exchanging of keys felt like a natural progression.

We also have toothbrushes and a few toiletries at each other's places, as well as some clothes.

The day we decided and followed through on all that, I felt so fucking good.

I am clearly really into this woman.

Guess that's why I'm smiling my ass off as I trot down the stairs to greet her.

"Hey." Cricket gives me a cute little wave.

"Hey, back at you." I reach her and take her into my arms.

"Mmm…" I trail my nose along her hair, which is pulled back into a long ponytail. "You always smell so delicious."

Hugging me tightly, she says, "Delicious, huh? Maybe later you can take a bite. You know, just to see if I taste as good."

Laughing, I lean back. "There are no maybes about it, babe. You do taste fantastic." I playfully smack her ass, and tell her, "But for now, let's get started on painting. Before I change my mind and scrap the whole project."

"Okay, okay," she says, laughing.

She looks so cute and sexy in black leggings and a pink long-sleeved sweatshirt with one shoulder pulled down, revealing a white tank underneath.

I come so close to just saying "Fuck it" to the painting.

But tomorrow I have an afternoon game, and the day after that we hit the road for a stretch of away matchups, mostly in the eastern part of the country.

So yeah, this is our best chance to get the painting done.

I'm glad it's only midafternoon. We'll have the whole rest of the day and the night ahead of us.

That means I will indeed be taking a "bite" of this hot and sexy woman at some point in time.

For now, though, I take her hand and say, "Come on. Let's paint."

Sighing, Cricket allows me to lead her down the long hallway to the first floor spare bedroom that'll soon be my home office.

The space is cleared out, and I laid down several drop cloths earlier.

I have two cans of teal paint set out, one on either side of the room, and two rollers. I also have an assortment of brushes in different sizes, mainly for edging.

Glancing around, Cricket notes, "This room really is a blechy yellow. I can see why you want to change it."

"Right?" I chuckle as I grab a screwdriver off the floor so I can pop open our paint cans. "I just couldn't picture myself sitting at a desk in here, working on the computer, surrounded by boring banana-colored walls."

"No, I can't see that, either," she agrees, laughing along with me as she picks up two wooden paint stirrers, one of which she hands to me.

Gesturing to the second can as I pop off the top, she says, "Pass that over when you're done and I'll start stirring."

"You got it."

Once the top is off, I slide the can over to her.

As she begins stirring, she remarks, "Wonder what this room was before?"

I blow out a breath and recall what I was told. "I think the realtor mentioned that it was a kid's bedroom."

Still blending the paint, Cricket glances around. "That kind of explains the pale yellow, I guess."

As I begin stirring my own can of paint, I raise a brow. "I know, right? You see why I need to change it then?"

"Aww," she coos. "But you'd look so cute. Like you said, a big, beautiful blond man tapping away at the computer, getting work done, surrounded by kid-yellow walls. All you'd need would be a few stuffed animals to complete the adorable picture."

I bark out a laugh. "Ahh, yeah, no, that's not happening."

Getting back to the task at hand, Cricket asks, "Okay, so where do you want me to start?"

"Anywhere is fine."

She nods, glancing around. "I think then I'll start with the corners. I like working with the brushes better, and I'm good with detail work."

"Perfect." I nod. "I'll grab a roller and get started on the walls."

Cricket kneels in the corner closest to me, adjusting the drop cloth. "Sounds like a plan," she says.

We're about to get to work when I realize something. "Hey, we can't paint in complete silence."

Cricket, having just dipped a brush into her can, looks up at me. "Some music would be good. Do you have a radio?"

"I have something better. Hold on a sec."

I run up to my bedroom to retrieve a Bluetooth speaker.

Once I'm back in the room with Cricket, I take out my phone. "We can stream one of my workout playlists."

"Ooh, I like that idea. I'd love to know what you listen to when you're skating and working out."

"You're about to find out," I tell her, smiling as the devices connect and I turn up the volume.

The yellow room is filled with the eerie opening chords of Disturbed's version of "The Sound of Silence."

"Oh my God, I love this song!" Cricket exclaims.

She begins humming along and painting in rhythm with the tune.

Softly, and really to myself, I murmur, "See, we really are fucking meant to be."

I guess she hears me, as she stops what she's doing and peers over.

I just shrug, because it is what it is—I am way into her, and there's no secret about it.

Has there ever been?

"Do you mean that?" she asks.

"I do," I reply. "It's the way that I feel. I have from the start. And it's only grown stronger the more we hang out." I pause, then ask, "Is that okay?"

Smiling, she tells me, "It's more than okay, Landen. I'm kind of right there with you, anyway."

I raise a brow. "You are?"

"Yes."

Quickly, she turns back to the wall and starts painting again.

Still, I can see that woman is smiling like crazy.

Hey, I'm grinning like a fool as well.

I get started with the roller, and it all goes smoothly from there. It's just us painting and listening to good music.

About an hour into it, I decide for sure that we're an amazing team in so many ways. We even have this tandem painting thing down.

As the music changes from song to song—some metal, some rock, and a little bit of pop—the walls transform from yellow to teal.

"It's really looking good in here," I say as I finish with the last of the walls.

"It is," Cricket agrees, leaning back to take a look around. "I love this color."

She's up on a small wooden ladder, finishing up with the last of the corners by the ceiling.

As she gets back to work, the pulled-down shoulder of her sweatshirt slips a little lower, exposing the part of her tank that's covering her breasts.

Holy shit, I don't think she has on a bra.

Kill me now.

I put the roller down in the paint pan.

Striding over to the ladder, I grab hold of a rung near her beautiful breasts, her warmth radiating.

I'm truly going to die if I don't touch her.

"What are you doing?" Cricket asks, pulling in a breath.

Gently, I take the paintbrush from her hand.

"I think this can wait," I say as I place her brush across the flipped-over lid to her paint can.

Turning my attention back to her, I murmur, "But I can't."

My hands find purchase on her waist as I urge her to come down.

As she wraps her legs around my torso, I grab hold of her ass.

With both of us laughing, I spin her around—once, twice—but then I stop.

"I have to kiss you," I tell her.

She touches her forehead to mine. "I feel the same way. So kiss me,

Landen."

I don't know if it's me who leans in or if it's her.

I think it's both of us as our lips crash together.

But it's definitely me who pulls her sweatshirt over her head, tossing it aside and lowering her to the drop-cloth-covered floor.

Propping up on my elbows above her, I say, "You have the cutest little streak of teal right…here." I touch her cheek where a smudge of dried paint is indeed smeared.

I then kiss the spot.

When I rise back up, Cricket trails a finger along my arm. "You have a little paint here too."

"I do?" I look down.

"Yes."

Lifting up from the floor, she presses her lips to the curve of my bicep, where there is a touch of teal. The dried paint extends up under the arm of my T-shirt.

Cricket lifts the material to kiss and lick.

"Fuck. Hold up a sec." I stop her long enough to tug my tee over my head.

As I ball it up and throw it aside, she traces circles down my chest to my stomach.

"Find any paint there?" I tease, raising a brow.

"No. But I could."

"How do you mean?"

I'm curious as to where this is heading.

I find out quickly when she reaches over to where I placed her paintbrush and dips her fingers into the wet paint on the bristles.

Pulling back her hand and holding her paint-soaked digits within inches of my chest, she says, "Now where should I start?"

Before I can say "Anywhere you fucking want," Cricket begins tracing circles again, spiraling teal paint over my pecs and down my abs.

Fuck, her touch feels amazing.

I don't even care that she's getting paint all over me.

It's latex.

It'll wash off.

In fact, we can clean up together in my shower later.

Maybe I can make that fantasy from long ago come true?

I interlock our hands, wet paint coating my palm and fingers.

With my clean hand, I pull up her tank, exposing her beautiful full breasts.

"I can never get enough of these," I murmur as I dab paint onto one nipple and then the other, trailing my finger down her taut tummy and leaving my mark.

Cricket groans and writhes, and I use the opportunity to wiggle her leggings and panties down and off.

She ditched her flats a while ago, and I sit up to slip my old running shoes and socks off.

"Those sweatpants have to go too," she demands.

"I'm on it, beautiful."

When I tug my sweats down my legs, my cock, hard as fuck, springs free.

"Mmm, going commando today, I see." She nods approvingly. "I like it."

"I bet you do," I reply, smirking.

Our eyes meet and I know it then—today is the day that I will finally have Cricket Nance, and she will finally have me.

I stop playing around with the paint, and I'm back on her in an instant. This is important, and I want to remember every second of it.

Licking her lips, she opens her legs.

I settle between them, brushing back a strand of hair that escaped her now-messy ponytail.

Our bodies press together tightly, the paint that hasn't dried smearing and covering our skin with every move.

I blow out a breath. "Fuck. This is kinky."

"Yes," Cricket groans. "I love it."

"I do too," I admit.

We can't stop writhing and rubbing.

Our skin grows more heated, my cock stroking her soaked folds and swollen clit with every pass.

Faster and faster, our hands are everywhere as we become desperate—for each other, for release, for *more*.

With Cricket's hand on my cheek, she whispers, "I want to feel you, Landen. *All* of you. I'm done waiting."

"Hell, I am too."

Growling, I reach down and adjust my dick so I can slip into her.

When I do, *fuuuck…*

I have to stop to just fill her *and* feel her.

Moving her hand down to my chest, she rasps, "Don't move. Stay just like that."

"Okay."

She begins working herself on me, arching her hips, sliding along my cock.

"Shit, woman."

"Right?"

She smiles up at me.

And then her eyes close as her brow furrows and she falls apart.

"Yes." I smooth back more loose strands of hair. "Come for me. Just like that."

As she quivers and spasms, I lower her hips and pick up the pace, fucking her hard and fast.

Her orgasm starts to subside, but then resumes.

"Jesus."

This is my undoing.

Feeling Cricket come and come again on my cock pushes me over the top.

Filling her, we collapse into the drop cloths, spent and satiated.

14

STAKE MY CLAIM

CRICKET

"**S**o Landen and I did the deed," I say to Bettina over the roar of the arena crowd. "And it was super kinky and hot as hell."

We're up in a luxury box. My boss, Ahren, really came through on the Wolves tickets today. Maybe that's due to the fact this is an afternoon game. They're not as popular as the night ones.

It's been really good, though.

We're up 4-3 late in the third.

Well, since Jaxon Holland just scored a goal, make that 5-3.

That's why everyone is going crazy.

But it's what just came out of my mouth that has Bettina almost dropping her hot dog.

Readjusting and saving a jalapeño from falling off the big pile on the top, she lowers her food and says, "Holy hell, what did you just say? Cricket, you sneaky little bitch."

After the sirens and lights die down, I murmur to her calmly, "You heard me."

There are other people in the box with us, but they're all a few rows back.

Still, Bettina keeps her voice low like I did when she replies, "Hot and kinky, huh? I'm going to need details on that. And now that we're on this subject, it's about damn time, woman! But what's with the delay in sharing? Why are you keeping this all to yourself?"

"I'm not. I'm telling you now." I shrug. "It just happened yesterday."

My friend looks confused. "Wait. I thought you two were busy painting."

"We were." Looking over at her, I wink. "But then we got busy doing *other* things. That's where the kinky part came in. Just think paint and sex and sticky bodies…" I let out a little squeak.

Wistfully, Bettina murmurs, "Ahh, I can only imagine."

"Imagine more." I give her a wry smile. "Then you might be semi-close to how fucking hot it was."

Bettina makes a face. "Shit, I hate you. Wild paint sex with that sexy man? You are one lucky bitch."

I assure her, "Aw, I'll find you a hot man to have wild paint sex with. I promise."

Crossing her fingers, she says, "I hope. And I'm holding you to that, by the way."

"Don't worry, I will," I assure her.

"So tell me about the hot paint sex," she says. "Was it all pretty much perfect?"

"For the most part. But cleanup was a bitch."

She laughs. "I'm sure it was."

"It did lead to some *really* good shower sex," I share.

Bettina nudges my shoulder. "So Landen is that good, huh?"

Sinking down into my seat, I giggle. "Is he ever! Apart from the kinky paint part—and that was amazing—the man is just as skilled with his cock as he is with his hockey stick."

As if to underscore my point, at that exact moment, Landen goes on a breakaway.

"Mmm, whaaa…" I can't even speak, so I just grab Bettina's arm.

Suddenly alone in the defender's zone, Landen pretends to wind up, but changes tactics at the last second and backhands the puck into the net.

"Holy hell, he just beat the opposing team's goaltender, and so damn easily."

Bettina grins. "Looks like Landen is scoring all over the place lately."

I can't argue that, and I nod excitedly. "You better believe it. And after that sweet freaking goal, he'll be scoring again later tonight as a reward."

That makes my friend laugh.

Oops, someone a few rows back overheard me. I hear snickering.

Oh, well, who cares?

My relationship with Landen is no secret. Even Ahren knows, and she's cool with it.

A few local hockey bloggers have also caught us out. There are pictures on their sites of us at dinner and dancing at a club.

I'm just happy the Wolves' organization has no problem with our dating.

"So what's next for you two?" Bettina asks.

"What do you mean?"

"I'm asking how serious is it getting? It's been a couple of months of seeing him all the time, right? So do you think there's a future with this guy?"

I think about it and reply honestly, "I do. I have from the start. But spending time with him has only solidified my feelings…and his."

Bettina then asks, "Have you guys said 'I love you' yet?"

I shake my head. "No."

"*Do* you love him, Cricket?"

Do I?

I blow out a breath and realize, "Damn, I think I do."

"Think? Or know?"

With certainty, I say, "I know I love him. It feels amazing to say it out loud. Maybe it is time for me to tell Landen, to let him know just how deeply I feel for him."

Bettina's clearly on board. "Yes! Let him know. What's the holdup?"

"I don't know." I shrug, feeling uncertain all of a sudden. "Maybe I shouldn't rush saying it. I think I'll just wait until the time is right."

"Do what you want," Bettina says, taking a bite of her jalapeño-laden hot dog. After she's done, she adds, "I wouldn't wait too long, though. You should let Landen know where your heart is. In doing so, you'll stake your claim."

"Stake my claim?" I murmur as the horn sounds and the game ends with a Wolves victory.

As Bettina and I stand, readying to leave, I think about how I do kind of need to stake my claim.

That's it.

I'm telling him.

No more waiting.

Landen needs to know how committed I am, and that I do love him.

Before someone else swoops in and lures him away.

15

THE L-WORD

LANDEN

I score a goal on a beautiful breakaway shot, and we ultimately win the game.

The best part of my day, though, is afterward when Cricket comes over to my house.

Not only does she look adorable in a cute floral sundress, but the way her long blonde hair flows down her back makes her extra sexy tonight.

I suggest we eat right away so I don't devour *her*.

Yeah, I'm saving that for later.

Since she informs me that she's really hungry—"I ate nothing at the game with Bettina, even though she had a hot dog"—I get right to work on grilling burgers.

While I'm out on the back patio, flipping meat patties, she throws together a quick pasta salad in the kitchen.

Since it's a pretty February day in Las Vegas—not too hot, not too cool—we decide to eat out on the patio.

We set up at the little iron table in the back.

"It's so pretty out here," Cricket says, gesturing to my landscaped gardens and the desert expanse behind where my property ends.

"Yeah." I nod, swallowing a bite of burger. "I like that it's not developed much at all. That's why I chose this particular house."

Leaning forward, she adjusts the umbrella above us so that the sun's not shining right into our eyes. "Well, I'd say you chose wisely."

She adjusts her cool mirrored sunglasses, and we dive into our food.

It amazes me that even doing the simplest things with Cricket, I have the best time.

I guess that's why I want to be around her as much as possible.

What does that mean, though?

Hmm, I need to think about that one.

I kind of already know—the answer on how I feel about her starts with a big ole letter L.

But feelings like that require serious talks and even more commitment.

My brain is quick to remind me of how I played it this way.

You wanted to date her exclusively, right?

Hell, you even have clothes and shit at each other's houses.

Plus keys!

You were onboard with all of that.

Where did you think all this would lead?

True, true, it's all fact.

But am I really ready for the next step?

Good question.

We've jumped over so many "firsts" and gone right to this.

It was by my design, of course.

And I take full responsibility.

Still, I have to wonder.

Did I make the right choice when I won that bet and asked Cricket to see me and only me?

Like from date number one?

And I vowed not to see other people.

Hmmm…

Was it too much, too fast?

It's a little late now, Landen.

Cricket pulls me from my confusing reverie when, after clearing the dishes and taking them inside, she returns and sits back down, and then asks, "Hey, where are you? You look like a man with a lot on his mind. You've been this way too, through most of the meal."

Waving my hand, I try to dismiss her accurate observations. "No, no, there's not that much on my mind. I was just thinking over a few things."

"Yeah, like what?" Smiling, she reaches over the frosted glass top of the wrought iron table and covers my hand with hers. "Were you reminiscing about that awesome goal you scored at today's game? Because let me tell you, Landen, that one was something."

I chuckle, happy as hell to think about something other than my errant musings. "It was pretty sweet, huh?"

"Pretty sweet?" Cricket pulls her hand back so she can reenact my backhand shot. "Whoosh! Score! That was more than pretty sweet, my beautiful man. That goal was freaking perfection."

I shake my head, peering down at the tabletop, a little embarrassed by her gushing.

Truthfully, I feel guilty for the thoughts that were just running through my mind.

You care about her, so stop it!

I shut my inner voice up and just murmur, "Wow, thanks, babe."

"Landen, I'm serious."

"I know you are."

Shit, I can't say it, not now, but what's "perfection" is having the woman you love be your biggest cheerleader.

Fuck, I just said the L-word.

Not out loud but in my mind.

Still.

Damn, I really need to get my head straight.

I'm everywhere yet nowhere.

Ugh!

"Landen…" Cricket waves her hand at me. "I feel like I'm losing you again."

"Sorry. I was just, uh… I was thinking about how it's going to suck to be on the road for the next week and a half."

Hey, at least that much is true.

"I know." She cringes. "It'll be the longest we've been away from each other since we met."

"I know, right?" I shake my head, dismayed.

Despite my sudden uncertainty, I really don't want to be away from her.

What if it makes things worse?

What if time apart causes me more confusion?

"It sure is going to blow," I mumble.

"Aww…" Cricket cocks her head, and damn, she is stunning. This woman takes my breath away—always. "So you're saying that you'll miss me?"

It's the total truth when I reply, "More than you could ever imagine."

Our eyes meet then, her azures to my greens.

There's so much more I want to say.

But I've never been the best talker.

Still, I can take her hand.

So I do.

I can also stand and lead her into the house.

I do that too.

"Do you want to go up to my bedroom?" I ask when we reach the stairs, my voice a silky whisper.

She nods.

Cricket is often the aggressor, which is totally fucking fun, but tonight I want to be the one in charge. If for nothing else but to assure myself that every decision I've made up to this point has been the right one.

Taking control, I sweep her off her feet.

Like literally, I lift her into my arms and carry her up the stairs.

Giggling, Cricket buries her face against my neck. "Damn, Landen, I'm missing you already."

Kissing the top of her head, I tell her, "That's why I'm going to give you some amazing sex to live on for the next several days."

She leans back, peering up at me as I stop on the landing.

"You always give me amazing sex," she says. "But hey, I'm up for more."

I dip her down so she can feel how fucking hard I am. And then I say, "I am too, babe. You feel how much?"

"Mmm, Landen… You better get me into that bed of yours as fast as you can."

I laugh, feeling better about things already. "Your wish is my command."

In the bedroom, my clothes are flying.

But I insist Cricket lose only her panties.

I tell her, "I want to fuck you with that dress on."

She does me one better.

Standing before me, not only does she slip off her panties, but she somehow manages to ditch her bra with her dress on, leaving the top buttons undone in the sexiest possible fucking way.

"You must be trying to kill me before I leave," I tell her gruffly.

She shrugs. "No. I'm just trying to be a little creative."

"Well, it's working. And for the record, I fucking love creative."

"Hmm, I bet you do."

"Enough talking."

Ever so gently, I lay her down onto the bed.

I want to go slowly for now.

There'll be time for desperate and frantic later.

Lifting the floral material of her dress, I kiss my way up one inner thigh, then switch to the other, kissing higher and higher.

Cricket is breathing hard, trying to remain still.

When I reach her already wet pussy, I lift her up by the ass and lathe my tongue along her folds.

Once, twice, again and again, like she loves.

I tease at her clit with little circles, taunting her with the promise of more.

She groans and writhes against me, urging me to finally suck her nub into my mouth and stroke it with my tongue.

Spasming, she comes hard.

I'm ready to climb up and enter her, but she makes me stop.

"No," she says, "it's my turn now."

Shit, I'm not saying no to that.

I flop over onto the bed, and she rises up to her knees.

Leaning down, she takes me into her mouth.

"Jesus."

Cricket works me to the edge but never over the brink.

I close my eyes and just enjoy, loving the feel of her mouth, her tongue.

When she stops, I don't have to wait long before she climbs atop me.

When I open my eyes, I see that she's unbuttoned her dress all the way.

God, she's sexy.

Her beautiful breasts are spilling out, so I reach up to massage the soft mounds.

"You look so beautiful on top of me like this," I tell her.

Smiling but saying nothing, she lowers herself slowly down onto my cock.

We both gasp once I'm fully sheathed inside.

"I may look beautiful, Landen, but you *feel* beautiful," she murmurs.

Reaching up, I cup her cheek and profess, "I fucking love you. You know that already, though, right?"

Whoa, where did that come from?

Did I just say that out loud?

I guess I did since Cricket has frozen atop me.

Shit, I feel her now more than ever. And she feels more amazing than before.

Is it because I've just admitted what's in my heart?

She sucks in a breath.

I feel that too.

She then says softly, "I love you too, Landen. I truly do."

We both breathe out then.

And it's okay.

I do love her.

And she loves me.

So loving each other is what we do late into the night.

16

I MISS HIM

CRICKET

Morning comes way too soon.

As the dawn light pours in through the blinds that we forgot to close last night, Landen's alarm blares to life.

"Ugh, no," I groan, rolling toward him. "I don't want you to go. Just stay."

After turning off the annoying beeping, Landen wraps me up in his arms.

Nuzzling my neck, he says, "I wish I could, babe. I'd like nothing more than to hang out with you all day in bed. But sadly, duty calls."

"I know." I sigh. "You go do your hockey thing and score lots of goals, okay? Make me proud."

Chuckling and holding onto me a little more tightly, he says, "That's the plan."

We kiss for a minute or two, but quickly realize there's no time for more.

Hopping out of bed with a disappointed growl, Landen prowls like a panther naked to the bathroom.

God, he is so damn hot when he's fired up.

I like primal Landen.

He's like a big blond lion.

And he's all mine.

I know that now, as we've both said "the words."

Bettina will be so happy.

I sigh, giggling as I snuggle down into the blankets and think about last night.

As I hear the shower turning on, I grumble, "I sure am going to miss that man."

The only saving grace is that I'll be busy too.

My hectic schedule starts right away—I have a promotional event today.

I pick up my phone from the nightstand and check my messages for any changes in the itinerary.

There is one.

"Oh," I murmur as I read the email from the team. "It looks like Blake Cavaletti and I will be heading over to the grade school. He'll be the one giving a talk to the kids and passing out autographed photos."

The original plan was for a minor "scratched" player to go with me. But clearly since Blake has become available, the team has assigned him to me.

Hmm, but why exactly is he available?

I discover as I read on.

The email informs me that Blake's not going on the road trip due to a minor injury he sustained during yesterday's game.

I tap the phone to my chin.

Now that I think about it, I do recall Landen mentioning something wasn't quite right when Blake came into the locker room after the game.

"He was definitely limping," Landen told me.

I grimaced, replying, "I hope it's nothing bad."

He assured me it probably wasn't.

I'll have to tell him it's obviously more than nothing if it's keeping Blake at home.

I have to admit, though, that I'm thrilled Blake is doing the promo event. The kids will be so much more excited to get to interact with a top player.

And speaking of the event…

I check the time.

Eek, I have to meet Blake in an hour and a half.

As soon as Landen comes out of the bathroom, I inform him of the update on his teammate.

I then throw on one of his discarded tees and start to rush into the bathroom.

But Landen stops me.

"Whoa, hold up there a sec." Clad only in a fluffy white towel—*sigh*—he slides his hand up under the oversized tee and grabs my ass. "Thank fuck Cavaletti has a wife he loves and adores. I can trust him to not be trying for a piece of this."

He squeezes one butt cheek, and I assure him, "Don't worry. I'm all yours." I start into the bathroom, Landen's hand slipping away as I coo, "And it's all because I love you."

As I close the door, I expect to hear it back—those words flowed so freely from his mouth last night—but I don't.

Maybe I just don't hear him.

I'm sure we're okay.

The only thing that strikes me as odd is when I'm out of the shower, Landen is gone.

On the nightstand is a note.

"Well, at least there's this," I mumble dejectedly as I sit on the edge of the bed, adjusting the towel wrapped around me and read.

> *Gorgeous, I am going to miss you so fucking much. Sorry I had to run, but the charter flight is super early. Wait, that's not entirely accurate. To be honest, I was worried I wouldn't want to leave if I stuck around.*
>
> *We'll talk and text a bunch, but it won't be the same.*
>
> *Love you,*
>
> *Landen*

Hmm, okay, so he did write that he loves me in the note.

That's a positive.

Still, it would've been nice to hear it from him directly, especially since I won't see him for days.

"Just stop it, Cricket," I admonish. "You're worrying too much about stuff."

Setting my concerns aside, I get dressed, choosing a smart black pantsuit and kitten heels.

And then I head out.

I have to stop at my own place to pick up some paperwork for today's event.

After I do that, I'm off to the Desert Sports Complex, where the Wolves play.

I meet up with Blake in the players' parking lot as planned.

He's driving a black Lamborghini when he pulls in.

Once he steps out of his car, limping slightly, I head over to him.

Nodding to his vehicle, I say, "What is it with you hockey players? Must you all own fancy sports cars?"

He laughs. "That's right. Landen has a Ferrari and a Porsche. I guess we just like to go fast…on the ice and off."

I think about my time with Landen driving the Ferrari out in the desert and how freaking fun it was.

"You know," I say, nodding. "I totally get that."

He raises a brow. "Have you driven one of Landen's cars?"

"Yep, the Ferrari," I reply.

"No way." Blake looks surprised. "He must really be into you, Cricket. No one—and I mean no one—ever touches that man's babies."

I want so badly to tell Blake that Landen is more than "into me," but I ultimately decide he can share that with his friend.

Not to mention, something still feels off about Landen leaving only a note and not saying goodbye, or that he loves me, in person. Especially after the night we had.

Add in the fact that he'll be gone for a while, and yeah, this sucks.

Shaking my head, I ask Blake, "Are you ready to go?"

He nods. "Yeah, let's do this."

As we begin walking over to my car, my sensible silver sedan, I joke, "Sorry you'll be stuck in this boring old thing today."

Part of my job as event coordinator is to sometimes transport players to the event, especially if there's only one like today.

Blake laughs. "That's fine. It's still a nice car."

"Ha!" Now it's my turn to chuckle. "It's okay, but it's no ritzy sports car."

Even he has to concede, "No, it's not."

Once we're in my car, I ask how he's feeling.

"Good," he says. "It's not a bad sprain. I should be back on the ice in no time. This is just a precaution."

"Thank God it's not bad, huh?" I plug the directions to the school into the GPS system.

"Yeah, definitely," he agrees.

It only takes us about fifteen minutes to get to our destination. The principal is outside waiting for us, and after exchanging pleasantries, she leads us to the auditorium where the event will be held.

The kids are already inside, so we go in through the back.

With the stage set up, I head out to the podium and say a few words.

I then introduce Blake.

He cracks a few jokes—clean ones, of course—and goes on to talk a lot about hockey and the importance of following your dreams.

The kids love him.

There's a Q&A afterward that I run, and then Blake and I pass out autographed photos.

All in all, the event is a raging success.

That's why I'm happy to discover, once I'm back in my office at the Desert Sports Complex, that I have more events coming up this week and next.

"This will keep me busy while Landen's away," I murmur to myself as I print out my new schedule.

I'm happy, but I'm still counting the days till he returns.

I miss him so damn much already.

But what can I do?

Sigh.

SECOND THOUGHTS

LANDEN

From the time I leave my house to the moment the team and I land at our first destination city—Chicago—I feel weird.

It's like I'm having some kind of an existential crisis.

Fuck, my mind is filled with second thoughts.

It's kind of like yesterday but worse.

Now that I'm away, I'm more worried than ever that Cricket and I are moving *way* too fast.

We were quick before in our decisions, but it felt okay at the time.

Now, though, it's different.

It's like we've hit hyper-speed and there's no going back.

I think maybe our saying "I love you" to each other has freaked me out.

Dating exclusively is one thing, but putting *those* words out there is something else entirely.

It makes everything bigger, more official.

And it leads to more—like moving in, like m-m-marriage.

Fuck.

I absolutely do love Cricket, though.

And when she told me last night for the first time that she loves me, my heart soared.

So why is all this uncertain crap in my head?

I just don't know.

Maybe it's the extraneous stuff going on—like this road trip and how the hockey world is approaching the trade deadline.

I know for certain that the Wolves will be trading someone.

There's talk that they'd like to acquire a more skilled centerman for my line.

The guy we have is all right, but Blake and I would probably produce a lot more if we had someone better at center setting up plays for us.

Rumor is the Wolves are looking to acquire a guy named Sebastian Alderman. He's big and strong and quick on his skates. He makes a lot of good plays too. He's also known for being daring. He'll fight anyone, do anything. The dude is fearless.

I hope we grab him from the Panthers.

Since we're down a guy this road trip, I'd like to see him get signed quickly. He could join us right away since my linemate Blake suffered a minor lower body injury during that last home game.

He'll be okay to play in about a week, according to team doctors, but the powers-that-be felt it best to have him stay home.

That's why he ended up scheduled for the event today with Cricket.

Anyway, if we pick up Sebastian, it'd be great.

He plays center, where we desperately need him, but he can also fill in at right wing.

It'd be cool to have him fill in for Blake.

But I guess we'll see what happens.

For tomorrow night's game against the Blackhawks, Coach Townsend is having a guy from our farm league play Blake's position.

I have a feeling as soon as we acquire someone better, that dude will be sent down.

But enough about that…

The rest of this afternoon is shaping up to play out like a normal road trip day when we have no game.

And it does.

After we check into the team hotel, the guys and I grab a light lunch down in a conference room that's been set up special for us, observing all our dietary needs.

After lunch, we head over to the practice facility for some ice time.

That goes fine, as expected.

When practice has just about ended, I get word that a bunch of the guys are going out to dinner before hitting a local casino tonight.

I haven't played cards in a while, so I grab Benny Perry, who's part of the organizing group, before we get back on the bus to head to the hotel.

Pulling him aside, I ask, "Is it cool if I come along with you guys to dinner and the casino?"

"Hell, yeah, man." He raps me on the back. "The more, the merrier. I would've asked, but you've been with Cricket so much lately that I figured you'd given up on gambling."

"Pfft," I scoff. "Hardly."

"Good, then we'll count you in."

"Cool," I tell Benny.

Once I'm seated on the team bus, I have that weird trapped feeling again.

I dismiss it.

You're being stupid, dude.

Shaking my head, I call Cricket to see how her event with Blake went and to update her on my plans.

I'm sent to voice mail, though.

Damn, I really need to talk to her.

I'll feel better then, I know it. .

But I'll have to try her later.

For now, I just text my plans to her so that she's in the know.

Back at the hotel, after showering and dressing to the nines—we're always in suits when we go out like this on the road—my teammates and I meet in the lobby.

It's a good crew.

There's Benny, me, our captain Brent Oliver, Jaxon Holland, Nolan Solvenson, and a few of our fourth-line dudes.

One of the guys rented a shuttle to transport us to a steakhouse for dinner and then to take us to the casino afterward.

That's good.

This way we can have a few drinks and not have to worry about one of us driving a rental SUV or whatever.

It's also easier than hailing taxis.

Plus it's fun on the way to dinner. We're all able to talk and goof around.

Dinner is amazing, but we eat rather quickly.

I think we're all pumped up to do a little gambling.

After we arrive at the casino, just like back at home, we're escorted to a VIP room for high rollers.

I head straight to the blackjack table with Benny and Nolan, while the other guys opt for roulette and poker.

I don't know if it's because I'm missing Cricket, or if it's that I'm still stressed about our professions of love, but whatever the case, I find myself ordering whiskey on the rocks as my drink of choice.

I usually don't drink anything that strong, or at all, when I'm gambling. I like to stay sharp.

But tonight I feel like I need something to take the edge off.

My stress from earlier feels like it's coming back with a vengeance.

I sigh as the dealer, a guy with salt-and-pepper hair and a pudgy nose, passes out the cards.

I check my first hand—I have a king and a three of clubs.

"Hit me," I say.

Unfortunately, I'm dealt a nine of hearts.

I'm over twenty-one, so I fold, disgusted.

I finish my drink and hail a server over to order another.

The cute cocktail waitress who saunters up to take the order bats her long lashes at me.

"You got it," she says saucily once I tell her what I want.

Before she takes off, I ask, "Hey, what's your name?"

Softly, she says, "Alana."

"Ahh, Alana." I nod. "I like it. That's pretty."

"Thanks, Landen."

It takes me a few seconds, but then I have to chuckle. "How do you know my name?" I ask.

She places one hand on her hip. "You play professional hockey, right?"

"I do."

"Well, it just so happens that I *love* hockey. I follow all the teams and make a point to learn about lots of the players."

"Wow, I'm impressed."

And I am.

"You should be," she says. "But…" She glances around, quieting to a whisper. "I better get back to work. You want your drink still, right?"

"Yes." I nod and tell her, "Sure, go, go."

My gaze lingers appreciatively on how her short, flouncy black skirt swishes and sways along the backs of her thighs as she walks away.

The bounce of her auburn ponytail only adds to her cuteness.

I clearly am a sucker for girls with their hair in ponytails.

Just like Cricket when we first met.

Speaking of which, what are you doing, man?

Hey, there's nothing wrong with an occasional wayward thought… or a harmless appreciative glance.

But maybe there is because Benny, to my left, elbows me, and says, "Hey, I thought you and our event coordinator were an item?"

I turn to him, frowning. "We are. Why?"

"Oh, I don't know." He rolls his eyes. "Maybe it's just hard to tell when you're eyeing up other women. I mean, dude, your tongue's practically hanging out."

Bristling, I scoff, "It is not. And my interaction with her wasn't that bad. I was simply ordering another drink."

He levels me with a stern admonishing stare, and I have to admit that he's actually right.

But something about the fact I shouldn't be checking out, nor chatting up, other women, at least not that flirtatiously, is rubbing me the wrong way.

I guess that's why I suddenly announce, "Even if I were flirting, I don't see a ring on this finger." I hold up my left hand.

Benny just shakes his head. "Dude…"

The cute waitress returns, and I take my drink from her.

For reasons I can't even fathom, before she walks away, I ask her, "What time does your shift end?"

I hear Benny coughing pointedly from behind me.

Fuck him.

Smiling, she tells me, "I'm actually done in—" She takes out and looks at her phone. "—about three minutes."

"No way."

"Yes way," she replies.

I can tell she's interested, so I say, "That's fucking fantastic. Would you like to get out of here and grab a drink with me?"

Smiling at me big and wide, she says, "I'd love to."

"Great."

I gather my winnings, making a point to not look at any of my teammates.

I don't want to see the shock and disappointment on their faces.

Standing, I swiftly walk away from the blackjack table with Alana.

18

LITTLE THINGS

CRICKET

After the event with Blake, I decide to do something nice for Landen. His office furniture has all been delivered and set up, as well as his computer and peripherals, but he needs some basic supplies.

"I can take care of that," I say to myself as I head to the closest office supply store instead of straight home.

It doesn't take long to get to my destination.

After I park my car, I check my phone.

"Shit, I missed a call from Landen."

I knew I should've linked to Bluetooth in the car, especially since I forgot to take my phone off Silent mode.

I'm just not on my game right now.

I think I'm simply tired and missing Landen. Once I get home, I am so just crashing.

The good thing is that Landen did leave a text.

Phew.

Landen: Heading out with the guys to dinner and a local casino. I'll be in kind of late, but I'll call if that's okay. Hope your day went well with the event with Blake.

I text him back that it all went amazingly.

I also say for him to have fun.

And then I let him know, **Hey, I'm zonked. Still call if you want, but if I don't answer, it probably means that I crashed. I'll try to stay up, though. I need to hear your voice. Miss you so much. Love you. Talk soon.**

The phone remains silent.

I sit in the car for a few minutes to see if Landen will text back, but there's nothing.

Oh, well. I chalk it up to the fact that he's probably already out with the guys.

That's fine.

I hope he has fun.

I, however, have some shopping to do.

"You sure do," I murmur as I hop out of my car.

Once I'm inside the office supply store, I grab a cart and start down the aisles. I grab boxes of pens, pencils, a few notebooks, lots of file folders, a stapler, a box of staples, paper clips, and a myriad of other things I feel Landen may need for his home office space.

I also decide to pick up some art for his newly painted walls.

There are a couple of cool black-and-white cityscape scenes I come upon that I think will look great on the teal walls.

One is of New York City at night, and the other print shows Las

Vegas during the day.

Both are aerial-type shots.

And, more importantly, both have meaning. These cities represent where Landen once played—New York—and where he plays now—Las Vegas.

They represent his past and his present.

Hopefully the Vegas one is his future too…with me.

Even though the art pieces are just prints, they're in nice wooden frames that'll match the richly colored furniture in Landen's office.

They're perfect in so many ways.

I can't wait for him to see them.

All in all, I'm pleased with my purchases.

I think Landen will be too.

I like doing little things like this for him.

A store clerk helps me out to my car with all my many bags. He carries the prints, as well.

Once everything is loaded, I thank him and drive off.

As tired as I am, I still make a point to stop by Landen's to drop off all the stuff in his newly painted—*thanks to us, yay!*—home office.

It still smells so fresh and clean in the room.

I don't hang the artwork or put anything away.

I figure I can do all that later this week.

It's another task that will keep me busy.

And that's what this is all about, right?

Making sure time goes as quickly as possible over the next several days.

Yes, for sure.

That's why, once I'm finally home, I pretty much go straight to bed.

I keep thinking how one day is gone and in the books, and there are only eight more to go.

I try to stay awake for Landen's call, but it just grows later and later.

Where is he?

I come to the conclusion that he must be having a really good time with the guys.

That's cool, he needs to let loose a little now and again.

Despite my attempts to keep my eyes open, they close of their own accord.

And soon I am fast asleep.

19

POOR CHOICES

LANDEN

After Alana clocks out, she informs me that there's a small private bar in the back of the main casino.

"We can sit there, order drinks, and talk with some privacy," she says.

"Great," I reply.

That's all this is going to be, I remind myself. *I'll just sit with her and shoot the breeze for a bit. I simply need to blow off a little steam before tomorrow night's game.*

It's all harmless fun, right?

Though I do have to wonder what Cricket would think.

Would she be okay with me chatting up a cute cocktail waitress at the bar all alone?

She probably wouldn't be fine with it.

Me, I would be pissed as hell if she did the same.

So why am I doing this?

Shit, I don't know.

All I do know is that I keep walking, following Alana through the casino.

"You should be left alone at this particular bar," she says, peering back at me as we continue down a long corridor of slot machines and table games.

"Sounds good to me," I reply. "I've been in the clear so far."

Crap, I've spoken too fast. A group of young guys are descending on us, and they start asking for autographs and selfies.

I happily oblige while Alana hangs back and out of the way.

At one point, though, one of the guys motions to her and asks, "Is that cute chick in the cocktail waitress outfit your girlfriend?"

I shake my head. "No. We're just..."—*wait, what are we?*—"uh, friends," I lamely state.

Hell, we're not even that.

What *am* I doing?

Feeling suddenly guilty, though I've done nothing blatantly wrong, I wrap up with the guys, grab Alana's elbow, and move on.

"Sorry about that," she says as she leans into me so I can hear her over a slot machine that is just fucking going off. "I thought we'd make it to the bar free and clear."

"Eh." I shrug. "It wasn't your fault. It happens."

I realize then that my hand is still on her elbow, and also that we're walking kind of close, like a couple.

Quickly, I drop my hand from her arm and give us a little space.

I'm relieved as fuck once we finally make it to the bar in the back of the casino.

Alana was correct—it is indeed quiet.

There's an old man and a middle-aged couple drinking at the bar, and that's about it.

I suggest we head to a private booth in a back corner.

"Okay," Alana says quietly. "Though I'm sure we'd be fine at the bar."

I shrug. "I just feel better being out of sight."

She frowns on hearing that.

Moving more swiftly, we head to the secluded booth. I choose the side where the back of my head is to the bar.

That makes me less conspicuous.

Alana tells me she knows the bartender, and will go up and order our drinks. "That'll draw less attention," she says.

"Great," I retort as she readies to go up to the bar. I hand her my credit card and add, "Just have him put everything on my tab."

"Oh, okay, thanks."

"No problem."

"So what would you like?" she asks before walking away. "The same whiskey on the rocks you were drinking back in the private room?"

I nod. "Sure, that sounds good."

When she walks away this time, I don't watch.

Yeah, this is feeling more and more like a bad idea.

Maybe I'm just sobering up.

So what am I doing still sitting here?

I'm not married, true, but I am committed to Cricket.

So why am I seated at a quiet booth in the back of a bar with another woman?

Why am I making such poor choices?

I don't know.

But I do know one thing—*this stops now.*

Standing quickly, I walk over to the bar where Alana is ordering our drinks.

"Hey," I say, garnering her attention. "Just have the bartender cancel my order, okay?"

"Why?" she asks, looking disappointed. "He isn't even charging for the first round."

"That's okay. I just think it's for the best if I go."

"Um, okay. Here's your credit card." She hands me my plastic, which I pocket. Looking totally down and confused, she says, "Can you please tell me what I did wrong, Landen?"

"Nothing, I swear." I shake my head. "This just isn't a good idea, that's all. I have a serious girlfriend back home, one who I am totally in love with. So this doesn't feel right. It's not fair to you, either."

"All right." Alana sighs. "I understand. And for the record, Landen Zehner, you're a good man."

I scoff. "I don't know about that. But I'm trying and maybe getting a little better each day."

I am.

That's why I don't return to the private room to play any more blackjack. I've had enough gambling for the night. Not just with my money but with my life.

Heading straight to the lobby of the casino, I find the driver of the shuttle and make arrangements for him to run me back to the team hotel, where I can't get into any more trouble.

I plan to call Cricket first thing.

Even though I came to my senses before anything stupid went down, I fully intend to keep the events of this night to myself.

It doesn't matter, anyway.

Nothing happened.

Plus, the one good thing that came out of tonight is that it's made me realize what I want and who I truly love—Cricket.

Other than that, as far as I'm concerned, this is all a blip on the radar that never happened.

20

GAME NIGHT AND GAMES

CRICKET

I miss Landen's phone call—it comes in late at night—but he catches me first thing in the morning as I'm waking up.

"Hey, beautiful, what are you doing?" he asks, sounding cheerier than I think I've ever heard him this early in the day. "I leave for practice in a few, but I wanted to check in since I missed talking with you last night."

Yawning and stretching, I reply, "That's very thoughtful of you. As for what I'm doing, I'm in bed and just waking up."

"Ahh," he coos softly. "I wish I were there with you. We could usher in the new day properly, eh?"

I groan, thinking of all the ways we absolutely could do that if Landen were in my bed with me.

"Ugh, I wish you were here too," I say. "So…damn…much."

"We better change the subject," he replies softly. "I'm in the hotel lobby sitting on a couch. I'm by myself, but there are employees floating around. It'd be a little awkward to get aroused."

That makes me laugh. "Yes, I would think. I'll be good."

Clearing his throat, Landen asks, "So what are your plans for today?"

"Just work stuff."

"Do you have any events on the schedule?"

"Not today. I'm just going into the office." I prop a pillow up behind me and lean back. "There is an event tomorrow, though."

"Oh, yeah? What are you doing?"

I blow out a breath. "Well, I'll be taking a couple of the guys who are still in town over to the children's ward at the hospital."

"Ahh, that sounds nice."

"It should be." I pause, and then say, "Oh, and on a side note, I'm sorry I missed your call last night. I crashed kind of early."

"No worries," Landen says flatly.

I decide to hold off on telling him about the office supplies. I want them to be a surprise, especially the prints.

Sighing, I ask, "So how was your night out with the boys?"

Landen is oddly silent for what feels like a really long time, and then he says, "It was all right."

"Just all right? You went gambling, right?"

"Uh-huh." He clears his throat. "We did."

"Did you win anything?"

"No, I lost."

There seems to be a deeper meaning to his words, so I have to check, "Is everything okay? You sound kind of...off."

"It is, Cricket. Everything is fine." He sighs deeply. "Still, I just want to tell you that I'm sorry."

A sense of concern that something is wrong comes over me.

Tentatively, I ask, "Sorry for what exactly?"

Landen swallows hard. "For starters, I'm sorry for not saying 'I love you' before I left. I'm also sorry for not texting it to you yesterday. That was wrong and stupid of me. I do love you, babe. I love you a lot. I just got a little freaked out, is all. But I'm, uh, better now."

I'm elated at what he's saying, but I'm scared that he just admitted he got a little freaked out.

That's not good.

It confirms my fears.

And now I have to wonder. Is there more to this sudden realization of his?

No, he'd tell me if there were.

I'm just overreacting.

I'm sure of it.

Damn it, it's so freaking hard to communicate over the phone when you're missing each other so much.

We need to be in person.

Do we ever!

Sighing, I don't press and just say, "I love you too, Landen. I miss you so much."

He sounds desperate when he replies, "Fuck, I miss you too. I can't wait to hold you again in my arms."

"Among other things," I tease, trying to lighten the mood.

It seems to work, as he's in full fun mode when he replies, "You bet your ass, babe."

Ah, things are getting back to normal.

Cheerily, I tell him, "Just play good hockey and the time will fly."

"You'll watch the games on TV?" he asks, like there's any question about it.

"You know it. In fact, I already have plans for Bettina to come over tonight for a viewing party."

"Cool."

Just then I hear a few of the other guys in the background.

"Do you have to go?" I ask.

"I do." He sighs. "My teammates are coming down, and it looks like the busses are lining up to take us over to the practice facility."

I nod even though he can't see me. "Okay, I'll let you go."

"Talk soon?"

"You know it."

"Love you."

"I love you too, Landen."

We disconnect and I kind of sit quietly in bed, thinking and tapping the phone to my chin.

Despite the call ending on a good note, the nagging feeling that something was off returns.

Too bad I have no time to dissect and figure it out.

I need to shower and dress and get my butt to work.

So, tossing the phone aside, I get started on my day.

Bettina and I check again to make sure we're fully prepared for the game.

"Are the nacho chips and hot and mild salsas in there?" I call out from the kitchen, where I'm taking boneless hot wings out of the oven. "Also check for the queso. We must have that."

"Yes, yes, and yes!" Bettina yells back from the living room. "Didn't you see me grab the bags from the pantry, the salsas from the fridge, and the queso from the microwave?"

After setting the pan of dry rub wings on the counter to cool, I walk over to the doorway that leads from the kitchen to the living room.

Leaning against the jamb, I say, "No, I didn't see you. You must've done all of that when I was upstairs changing."

Work ran late today. When I arrived at my townhouse, Bettina was already outside waiting in her car.

We rushed in, and while she went to the kitchen, I made a beeline upstairs to change into comfy leggings and a black-and-red Wolves sweatshirt.

"Ah, yes," she says. "You were still up there now that I think about it."

"That's okay. It doesn't matter." I straighten and shrug. "What do you want to drink?"

"Diet Coke is fine."

"Cool." I turn back to the kitchen. "I'll grab a can for each of us."

I take in the cold colas and return to the kitchen to plate the wings.

I divide them as evenly as I can, grab a big pile of paper napkins, and then head back into the living room with essentials in hand.

"Here you go." I set Bettina's plate down in front of her on the coffee table. "Oh, wait, I brought napkins too."

I hand her a bunch, and she says, "Thanks, Cricket."

"Not a problem."

I sit down next to her and turn on the big TV on the wall.

"So the Wolves are playing the Blackhawks tonight, right?" she asks.

I pick up a chicken wing, blowing on it to cool it down. "Yes."

"And Landen's still on the third line?"

"Uh-huh." I take a bite of the wing.

"What's going on with the trade deadline? Does Landen have any inside scoop? Are the Wolves picking anyone up?"

After swallowing, I reply, "Yeah, I think so. He didn't confirm anything, but I heard a rumor today at the office that we're looking hard at Sebastian Alderman."

Bettina asks, "Who does he play for again?"

"He's with the Florida Panthers."

"Ah, that's right. I've been so busy with school and work that I've been slipping on keeping up with hockey-related things." She takes her phone from her gray hoodie pocket. "Let me look him up." As she starts tapping and scrolling, she murmurs, "Let's see, let's see…"

"You are so funny," I note, shaking my head.

But she's not laughing when she suddenly exclaims, "Holy crap! This dude is hot as hell. How have I never heard of him before?"

"Probably because he plays for a team on the other side of the country," I suggest.

"Yeah, maybe." She holds up her phone. "Here, check him out."

I take her phone and peer down at the image of Sebastian on the screen—his headshot from the Panthers' website.

"Wow, very nice."

Sebastian Alderman is one fine-looking man. He has coppery brown hair, deep brown eyes, and what looks to be a super-muscular build, based on his wide shoulders.

Nodding approvingly, I hand Bettina her phone back.

Staring down at the image of Sebastian longingly, she says, "When is the trade deadline again? Maybe you and Landen can set me up on a date with this dude. Then I too could have hot paint sex stories to tell."

She's totally kidding.

Or maybe not.

Laughing, I tell her, "Oh, stop. The deadline is tomorrow. If you're serious, let's see if this dude even ends up in Vegas. Okay?"

"Yeah, yeah, whatever." She waves her hand. "You're right. But if he does end up here…" She winks over at me with her big brown eyes. "… then I definitely want to meet him."

Laughing, I just shake my head and turn my attention to the TV.

I've had the pregame programming on mute, but the game is about to start. So I turn the sound back on.

The teams start coming out onto the ice.

Yes!

First up are the Wolves, to a chorus of boos.

The Hawks skate out next to barrage of cheers from their fans.

Not surprising since they're the home team.

As the game gets underway, Bettina and I feast on chips and wings.

The action is good. The Wolves end up pretty much dominating Chicago. Landen doesn't score any goals, but he does rack up an assist on a Nolan Solvenson goal after Coach Townsend changes up the lines.

By the time the third period is coming to a close—with a score of 6-1—Bettina is paying more attention to her phone than to the TV.

"What are you doing over there?" I ask as the horn sounds, signaling the end of the game, with a victory for the Wolves.

As I turn down the volume, she says, "I'm still looking at hockey stuff."

"Man, you really are into this Sebastian guy, huh?"

She looks over at me and rolls her eyes. "It's not just him that I'm checking out. Apparently there are a lot of other hot hockey dudes I've somehow neglected to notice."

"Mmmhmm," I agree. "I can't argue with the hot, hockey dudes observation. It's so true."

"Oh, jeez, you just mean your Landen. You are so into that guy that it's not even funny."

"I am," I confess, sighing wistfully.

"Okay." She focuses back on her phone. "Let's see what's online about him."

I snort, "Like I don't check the internet every day?"

"Yes, but I have a feeling you're not as thorough as I can be. Like, let's see if he's tagged in any random fan photos."

"Hmm, I don't ever really do that," I admit. "That's true."

"You should," she warns.

Still certain she won't find anything of interest, I mutter, "Sure, whatever. Do what you want. Knock yourself out."

I'm feeling pretty confident, until she's holding up her hand and exclaiming, "Whoa, wait a gosh darn minute here!"

"What is it?" I ask, my stomach churning.

Bettina bites her lip and holds the phone protectively against her chest.

Shit, this must be bad.

"Give me that," I demand, reaching for her phone.

"No, Cricket, no…"

Luckily, I'm quicker than her and in possession of her phone in an instant.

"Now let me see what's so damn inter—what the fuck!"

I'm rendered speechless.

Until I muster up enough righteous anger to grind out, "What the hell is this shit?"

What the hell is this shit is right.

Before me on the screen are photos of Landen—*my* Landen—hanging with some floozy cocktail waitress in a ponytail.

And they're in multiple locations!

I scroll and scroll.

He's walking with her through a casino, his hand on her elbow.

Oh, and here's one of him and the same girl in a cozy booth. It's taken from behind, but I can tell it's Landen.

Here's another where he's chatting with her in a bar, standing far too close for my liking.

"Out with the guys, my ass," I mutter bitterly.

No wonder Landen sounded so weird on the phone.

No wonder he called so super late.

And no wonder he was apologizing the next day.

Telling me he loves me was just his way of making himself feel better.

I'm sure of it.

God only knows what he did with this chick.

Softly, Bettina asks, "What are you going to do, Cricket?"

Crossing my arms, I reply resolutely, "That's easy. I don't play these kinds of games. I'm breaking up with the bastard."

FALLOUT

LANDEN

We play a great game and the Wolves win 6-1. But once I'm in the visiting team locker room, things start to go sideways.

First, I try to call Cricket and she doesn't pick up.

That's odd.

I know she's at home watching the game with Bettina, so this makes no sense.

So I send a text instead, indicating for her to call me.

I send another text immediately after, amending for her to wait a half an hour since I have to shower and get dressed.

I just don't want to miss her call.

But after I've cleaned up, dressed, and boarded the team bus that's now heading back to the hotel, there's still not one peep from Cricket.

No texts, no calls, no nothing.

Shit, I'm genuinely starting to worry.

Once I'm up in my hotel room, I try her again.

This time someone answers, but it's not Cricket.

It's Bettina.

"What?" she snaps.

Tentatively, not sure what the hell is going on, I ask, "Uh, can I speak to Cricket?"

Bettina grinds out, "Actually, no, you can't. She doesn't want to talk to you."

This is crazy.

What's going on?

"Why not?" I ask.

Bettina snorts. "Do you really need to ask such a stupid question? We saw the pictures of you, Landen."

I'm totally stumped. "What pictures of me?"

"The pictures of you and your little cocktail waitress friend. *Those* pictures. Ring a bell, buddy?"

My heart sinks. "Oh, fuck."

"That's right, dude. And for the record, Cricket doesn't care to see you, or talk to you, ever again. Unless, of course, it's in a strictly professional capacity related to the team. Otherwise, stay out of her life."

I run my hand down my face. "Bettina, it's not what it looks like. Can I please just talk to Cricket and explain?"

I hear her cover the phone and ask if she wants to talk to me.

I then hear Cricket responding with an adamant "No."

Damn, that woman is so stubborn.

But can I blame her?

I brought this on myself.

It was stupid to leave the private room with Alana, and even dumber to go to that bar with her afterward.

And though I left, the damage was done.

I know good and well that there are people everywhere with cameras in their phones.

What was I thinking?

I clearly wasn't.

I was too busy panicking about committing.

And now I got what I thought I wanted—I'm free.

But it turns out, that's actually the last thing I want.

I try again to get Cricket to talk to me, or FaceTime, or even text.

But she's adamant, as relayed by Bettina.

At some point, I get the impression Cricket has left the room.

That's the only explanation I can come up with for when Bettina states quietly, "Hey, for the record, I think you're an ass. But don't give up on her, okay? That is, if you really do love her, Landen."

"Bettina, I do. And trust me, I will *never* give up."

The trade deadline is the next day, and as expected, we pick up Sebastian Alderman in a trade with the Florida Panthers.

I find this out right before the team is boarding our charter plane to Detroit to play the Red Wings.

The Wolves didn't give up much, just our backup goaltender and a few low draft picks. Alderman is thirty, so his age probably factored in on that deal.

Hey, we're still the winners in the end—Sebastian is a really fucking good player.

He proves it the next night at our game in Detroit.

Even after flying in the night before, getting barely any sleep, and attending our early morning practice, he is still fucking on fire.

And the guy's not even playing his true position of center. He's filling in at right wing for Blake on my line, just as I suspected he would.

I am really impressed. Sebastian is amazing, a solid all-around good hockey player.

We're right now in our own end, digging for the puck in the corner.

It pops free, and a forward from the Red Wings tries to corral it.

Lucky for us, one of our defenseman checks him hard and knocks him right the hell off the puck.

It squirts free…to me.

Damn!

I see Sebastian is open at the blue line, so I pass the puck up to him.

Our team starts up ice, making our way into the defenders' zone in a perfect tic-tac-toe pattern.

It's like we're at practice, only this is for real.

I love that I have chemistry with this Sebastian dude already.

It bodes well for the future.

But now is what counts, so when he shoots the puck to me and I see a clear path, I slap-shot that fucker so damn hard.

Annnnd it goes in.

"Fuck, yeah!" I cry out.

I just beat the goaltender like he wasn't even there.

Sebastian and the other guys come over to celebrate with me.

There are high-fives and pats on the back, a few stick taps too.

Man, I feel good.

I hope Cricket is watching.

It hits me then—why would she watch this game?

She hates me now.

The woman won't even talk to me, for Christ's sake.

I'm doomed.

And just like that, my beautiful goal means nothing, making me realize a world without Cricket in my life is a fucking miserable place to be.

THE AFTERMATH

CRICKET

I stand strong in my decision to not have any further contact with Landen. It's the right thing to do, for me at least.

I just can't be with someone I can't trust.

And I can't trust him.

It doesn't mean I'm not miserable, though.

The day after our breakup, I'm just going through the motions.

I attend the event at the hospital with the two not-so-well-known players.

They're really quiet around me.

It's all "Yes, ma'am" and "No, Miss Nance."

Yeah, okay, all right.

Clearly the word has gotten out that Landen and I are done.

Amazing.

I swear hockey gossip spreads faster than wildfire.

There are no secrets in this league.

Case in point—Landen's little tryst in Chicago. It took less than twenty-four hours for me to find out about it. Thanks to Bettina, of course, and her superior sleuthing.

On the way home from the charity event, I consider stopping by Landen's to pick up my clothes and other things.

I'll leave him the office supplies.

I'm not that vindictive.

He can think of them as a parting gift.

But I'm sure as hell not setting anything up, nor will I be hanging those cityscape prints.

That crap can all stay in the bags and leaned up against his desk.

In the end, though, I just drive straight home.

I don't have it in me to step inside his house and not lose it.

And I've done enough crying for the day.

My eyes are wet even now.

Swiping at a traitorous tear streaming down my cheek, I pull into my driveway and cut the ignition.

Once I'm inside my place, I turn on the TV just to have some kind of sound in the background.

But shit, I forgot today is the trade deadline.

And the TV is tuned to the NHL channel.

Trades are being made all over the place.

Apart from the charity event, I've successfully avoided all things hockey today.

But I can't now.

A part of me just has to listen.

The commentator just announced the Wolves have picked up

Sebastian Alderman.

"That was to be expected," I murmur as I sit down on the sofa.

I may as well pay attention to the details.

I'll be working with this dude soon enough, right?

"Yep, I will."

Sighing, I turn up the volume.

Sebastian will be playing on Landen's third line at the center position. But since Blake is hurt and out, he'll be filling in at right wing for the remainder of the road trip.

"So Detroit should be interesting tomorrow night," the announcer says.

"It will," I agree softly.

The truth is, I can't help but feel excited for the game.

I want to see the new guy play, sure, but it's Landen I really long to watch.

He probably thinks I won't tune in, but he's so wrong.

It's just not that easy to move on.

The next day, after a long day of work, I don't invite Bettina over to watch the game with me.

But I do heat up the leftover wings from the other night.

"Not the most nutritious dinner," I mutter to myself, "but it'll do."

With a bottle of ranch dressing wedged in my elbow, to serve as a dipping sauce, I balance my plate of wings and a can of Diet Coke as I make my way to the sofa.

Success—I don't drop a thing!

After setting up my dinner on the coffee table, I turn on the game.

It's the end of the pregame, so the real action is about to start.

First, though, there's an interview on the ice with the new acquisition.

The reporter says, "Well, Sebastian, you've had quite an eventful twenty-four hours."

"I have," he agrees. "It's been wild."

"So tell us how you got word that you'd been traded."

Sebastian chuckles, the little crinkles at the corners of his deep brown eyes deepening and making him look quite handsome. "I learned about the trade yesterday morning when my agent called. Of course, there'd been chatter."

The reporter nods. "There always is. So what happened from there?"

Sebastian blows out a breath. "I pretty much grabbed a bag, threw some things in, and flew up to Detroit."

"Crazy! And you made it to practice this morning?"

He chuckles. "I did."

"That's fantastic. Do you feel ready to play?"

"I do. I'm super psyched to join the Wolves."

"Well, good luck tonight."

"Thanks, man."

Sebastian skates away, and that's when I catch sight of Landen. He's skating around with the other guys, warming up.

When he reaches the bench, he takes off his helmet to make an adjustment.

My heart skips a beat.

He looks so cute.

His blond hair is a bit of a mess like always, and he's biting his full bottom lip as he messes with the helmet.

Sighing, I close my eyes.

I have to, or I may do something stupid like call him and leave him a message that I changed my mind and have forgiven him.

But no, I can't.

I need to stay strong, no matter how hard it is.

And it's certainly not easy.

Yeah, no, it seems as angry as I am with Landen Zehner, the jerk still holds my heart.

23

CRICKET ON MY MIND

LANDEN

The rest of the road trip goes by faster than I expect it to, especially considering I don't join the guys in any more late nights out.

When there's no game or any practice, I just stay in my hotel room, reading and watching TV.

All safe things to do that keep me out of trouble.

At the end of the road trip, the Wolves finish with three wins and one loss.

Not too shabby, which is good since it's March and these games mean a lot. We're in playoff contention, but we need to stay sharp and on top of things.

Too bad I have one huge distraction—my promise to myself to win Cricket back.

I arrive home late on a weeknight, having flown in on the team jet from St. Louis, the last city we played in.

I drive from the airport in my Ferrari, thinking about the night Cricket and I took this car out to that desolate road in the still-wild parts of the desert.

She sure was wild that night.

The beauty of her coming apart, her glittery silver dress shimmering in the orange-y moonlight, fills my mind.

I knew I'd always remember her like that.

I just didn't know it'd be so soon and so bittersweet.

"I can change all that, though," I remind myself as I pull into my garage. "I can. And I will."

Since Cricket is on my mind so much tonight, once I'm inside the house, I stroll down the hall to the home office she helped me paint.

I need a reminder of that day and what it led to.

Jesus, it can't be over.

We've only just begun.

I can't believe it was only about ten days ago that we said "I love you" to each other.

Yet here we are.

That's when it strikes me that maybe her pulling away is her version of cold feet, not unlike what happened to me.

I mean, I know I was stupid. But why else would she not let me explain what happened in Chicago?

Why will she not see me?

"That has to be it," I murmur as I step into the home office.

It smells of fresh paint, and a hint of Cricket.

That makes me even sadder.

But I'm heartened when I turn on a light and find bags from an office supply store.

Cricket must've been here!

I quickly head over to check them out and find the bags are filled with items I can really use. There are also two framed pieces of what appear to be artwork leaned up against the desk.

They're turned the other way, so I have to spin them around to see what they're of.

Within seconds, I'm murmuring, "Wow, no way."

I slide down to the floor and just stare at the prints.

One is a black-and-white photograph of New York City and the other is of Las Vegas.

I know then that Cricket chose this artwork with me in mind.

It was only last summer I was traded from the Islanders to the Wolves.

And here I am now.

These prints represent the two most recent cities I've played in.

I stand then, peering at both prints before me and deciding which wall each will look best on.

"I wish Cricket were here to help me," I whisper.

I wish she were here for many more reasons than that.

But it would be nice to have her opinion right now.

I'm on my own, though, so I do the best I can.

I place the New York cityscape on the wall behind the desk and the Las Vegas one on the wall to my right. That way it'll be what you see first when you walk in the door.

It seems fitting, as New York is part of my past.

And Las Vegas is my here and now.

It's also my future.

But only if I can win Cricket back.

Otherwise, I'm going to ask to be traded.

I just can't live here without her.

24

WHAT FRIENDS ARE FOR

CRICKET

I immerse myself in my work, spending extra time at the office and going above and beyond with the events I work.

The next thing I know, the road trip is over and the guys are back in town.

That, of course, includes Landen.

Landen, who's left me numerous voice messages and texts, all apologetic and asking if I would please meet with him so we can "talk."

Ha!

He wishes.

I don't respond to a single message or text.

In fact, I'm pretty adept at avoiding him completely over the next week.

We have no events scheduled together—*thank God*—and I don't attend any of the games.

I do watch them all on TV, though.

And I keep wondering where we went wrong.

Why did Landen not say he loved me that morning?

And why was he freaking out?

Something was clearly wrong.

Did we move too fast?

Was that it?

Maybe, as why will I not let him explain himself?

Am I just being stubborn?

Or do I need space too?

"Ugh, I don't want to think about it," I cry out.

But I must.

First, though, I need a trusted friend I can confide in.

So for the next game, I invite Bettina over.

We watch the beginning in relative silence.

I think she doesn't know what to say.

And I'm thinking about stupid Landen.

But enough of that!

The minute the first intermission begins, I mute the sound on the TV.

"What's up?" Bettina asks, twisting to me.

She's a few feet away on the sofa.

Sighing, I share my thoughts on the demise of my relationship, everything I've been mulling over since the break-up.

Once I'm done pouring out my heart, she tells me that she has a theory.

"And just what is that?" I ask, propping a throw pillow under my elbow and turning to her.

She shrugs, like she has it all figured out and it wasn't that hard to do.

"I think you both just got cold feet. Things were moving way too fast."

"You're freaking nuts," I snort, not wanting to admit she's articulating what I've been secretly thinking. "That jackass cheated on me."

She tsks, "Now, now, you don't know that. From what I gleaned, after scouring practically the whole internet as it relates to hockey, nothing happened that night with Landen and that chick. He was just hanging with her. And yes, it was wrong and a stupid decision on his part. But it was basically harmless."

"Basically harmless, my ass!" I exclaim. "He shouldn't have been 'hanging' with anyone of the female persuasion. And did you see how he had his hand on her elbow, leading her all gently through the crowd?" I huff. "That was disgusting. Oh, and let's not forget the lovely photo of the two of them chatting in a bar all cozy-like. It makes me ill."

Bettina ignores my theatrics.

Still appearing thoughtful, she says, "True, it wasn't a good look. But if nothing happened—"

"Doesn't matter," I interject, cutting her off. "It's the principle of the thing."

"Is it really, though?" she asks softly.

I look down and twist at a loose thread on the throw pillow. "What's that supposed to mean?"

"It means I think you're the one keeping this going, Cricket. It's like you're pushing Landen away."

"Yeah, right," I murmur.

I'm resisting the truth. In my heart, I know she's right.

Good thing the girl is insistent.

"It's true," she goes on. "Didn't you tell me he's been leaving messages like crazy?"

"Texts too," I admit.

"See!"

"They've slowed down significantly," I throw out as a counterargument.

But Bettina isn't buying what I'm selling. "That's because you haven't replied to a single one, you goofball."

"Goofball?" I raise a brow.

"It's the nicest thing I could think of," she admits. "I have more colorful terms if you want to hear them."

"No, no." I cover my ears. "I can only imagine."

Scooting over, Bettina makes me lower my hands. "Hey, listen to me."

"Why?"

"Because this is what friends are for, to set your stupid ass straight when you're all over the place and screwing up your life. I know you love Landen. And he loves you. Mistakes happen, but love is worth fighting for."

"Why do you have to always make so much sense?" I murmur, giving in.

Smiling smugly, she picks my phone up off the coffee table and holds it out to me. "Here, call Landen."

I panic, shrinking away like the phone is toxic. "No, I can't do that. I'm, uh, not ready to talk to him yet."

"Will you at least text him, then? Just let him know you're willing to meet up and talk."

"I don't know," I mutter.

Bettina blows out a clearly frustrated breath.

And then she asks, "Do you still love him or not?"

I nod. "I do."

"Then I think you know what you need to do now."

I take the phone, albeit reluctantly.

And then I send Landen one simple text, one that reads **I'm ready to talk if you haven't given up on me.**

NEVER GIVE UP

LANDEN

After the game, I return to the locker room. It's pretty subdued since we lost.

Ah, but you can't win them all.

Yeah, I'm learning that.

Sadly, I'm starting to think I really may not be able to win Cricket back.

What else am I to believe?

After dozens and dozens of attempts to communicate with her, I think she truly might be done with me.

Maybe she never really loved me in the first place.

Damn, that hurts to think about.

No one in the locker room is in the mood to talk, and that's fine with me. I get undressed and secure a towel around my waist.

My phone is in my bag.

For the hell of it, I decide to check for messages from Cricket.

I expect nothing, but *whoa, wait!*

There's a text from her.

I can't believe it, so I have to read it, like, six times.

I'm ready to talk if you haven't given up on me.

Is she crazy?

Smiling so big that it hurts, I text her back that **I'll never give up on you, beautiful.**

She responds right away: **Do you want to come over and we can talk?**

Me: **Are you kidding? Just let me grab a quick shower and I'll head straight to your house. I'm in the locker room now.**

Cricket: **Okay.** And then: **Landen?**

Me: **Yes?**

Cricket: **I know we have a lot to talk about, but I need to tell you I've missed you like you wouldn't believe.**

Me: **Babe, you don't even know.**

Cricket: **Okay, I'll let you go so you can shower. I'll see you soon and we'll talk more.**

Me: **You got it.**

My heart is soaring.

I can't wait to see her.

Quicker than I ever thought possible, I toss my phone back in my bag, take a speedy shower, and get dressed.

My teammates are looking at me like I've just lost my mind.

Maybe I have.

I do feel a little unbalanced, but in a really good, happy kind of way.

Cricket is obviously giving me a chance to set the record straight.

At least, I hope that she is.

It's all I really want, a chance.

I bet I can make things right if she hears me out.

I think we both ran scared, and now we're coming together.

God, I hope we are.

With that in mind, I say goodbye to my teammates and practically run out to my car.

The drive to Cricket's townhouse is a blur.

I've never been so happy I have a really fast car.

I'm also pretty thankful that the roads aren't congested.

In what feels like no time at all, I'm knocking on the door to her place.

Though I still have a key, just letting myself in doesn't feel right.

We need to work back to that.

Like always, when Cricket opens the door, I'm in awe.

Even in drab gray sweatpants and a navy blue hoodie, with her honey blonde hair piled high on her head in a messy bun, she still has the power to take my breath away.

Before I can censor my words, I blurt out, "Baby, I love you."

Though she rolls her eyes, I catch her grinning. "Just get in here," she mutters as she tugs at my arm.

Hey, she's smiling and touching me. It can't be all that bad.

I let her lead me into her living room, where she gestures for me to take a seat on the sofa.

I plop down, adjusting my dress slacks.

I hate that I'm in fancy clothes—I have on a crisp white button-down in addition to the nice pants—and she's so comfy and casual.

It makes this all feel far too formal.

But as long as Cricket's comfortable, that's all that matters.

And she seems fine.

When she takes a seat in the chair beside the sofa, she curls her legs up underneath her.

Placing her elbow on the arm of the chair, she leans forward and rests her chin on her fist.

Big azure eyes meet mine as she says, "Thank you for coming."

"I'll always come for you, Cricket."

We can't help but smile at each other at the double meaning.

Looking away, she clears her throat. "Anyway, I think we should finally talk."

Blowing out a breath, I tell her, "That's all I've ever really wanted, a chance to explain my stupid behavior in Chicago."

She bites her lip. "Look, I know nothing happened, Landen."

"That's true. But my actions were dumb. I don't know what I was even thinking, hanging out with that girl. I clearly wasn't."

Sighing, she says, "I think I know why you did that, though. And I definitely know why I reacted the way I did, refusing to talk to you and not letting you come to me and explain."

I raise a brow and ask, "Can you tell me what that reason was?"

"Yes. We moved too fast, right from the start. It was too much."

"Wait, Cricket—"

"No." She holds up her hand. "Let me finish."

I'm sufficiently cowed, as I should be.

"I'm sorry for interrupting you," I murmur.

Softly, she reiterates, "We moved too fast, Landen. We did. Right from the beginning, when we agreed, as a result of you winning that bet—" Her eyes meet mine meaningfully. "—that we'd be exclusive."

"You're probably right," I grudgingly admit.

Cricket sighs. "I mean, it was kind of cool in a way, not dating anyone else, not even considering other possibilities. But it made us essentially boyfriend and girlfriend right away."

"It did."

"And then a little time passed and we said 'I love you.'"

She releases one long breath, and I do the same.

"True, we did. But…" I hold her gaze. "I meant it when I said it. And really, it wasn't right away. We only said the words before I went away on the road trip. That was well into our relationship, Cricket."

"Yes, but it suddenly put a lot of pressure on both of us on top of how we got started. Why else did you get cold feet?"

She's right, and all I can do is shrug.

She sighs, and then says, "I think on top of our fast start, it became too much. I mean, what's next, Landen? Marriage?"

She throws her hands up in the air.

But I just grin over at her.

"Landen, stop."

I concede. "Okay, okay. I'm only kidding."

"I know."

If Cricket believes I was only teasing—which I'm not sure I was—why does she look so sad all of a sudden?

Interesting.

I make a mental note to think on that later.

I remind myself that we still have a long way to go to get *there*.

Man, I think the only speeds I have are zero or one hundred.

Is it nuts that I'm actually considering it?

Marriage, that is.

Shaking my head, I put that out of my mind and say, "Okay, I hear everything you're saying, and you've made several valid points. Truth is, like I told you, I was feeling kind of freaked out, and I guess you could say I felt trapped. It all came to a head that night I hung out with the girl. Still, it was all of my own making. And you're right. I should never have made you agree to see just me and only me in the beginning. It put a lot pressure on both of us. Maybe we didn't see it then, but we sure see it now, don't we?"

"Yeah." She shrugs. "But I lost that bet fair and square."

Softly, I murmur, "Can I share something with you about that?"

She looks really curious as she says, "Of course."

"Even knowing what I know now, I'd still do it the same way all over again. I just don't think I could stomach the thought of you seeing other men."

Cricket rolls her eyes. "You would live."

Her comment makes me worry, so I ask, "Do you *want* to see other people now?"

Saving me from complete heartbreak, she thankfully says, "No."

"Thank God."

"What about you, Landen? Do you want to see what else is out there for you?"

That's an easy one to answer. "Hell no. I know what I want."

"Do you, though?"

"I do."

"Well, then I'm afraid you're not going to like what I have to say next."

My heart begins beating frantically.

Maybe Cricket was just punking me when she said she didn't want to see other people.

Fuck.

"What is it?" I ask warily.

Sticking her hands into the big middle pocket of her hoodie, she eyes me defiantly. "Okay, here are the new rules. I'll still date you, and only you. And the same goes on your side."

"You got it."

"But…" She holds my gaze. "I want us to take a step back. We need to start over in some kind of way, so we can get back to a good place. Can we do that, Landen?"

This doesn't sound so bad.

A little confusing, yes, but not bad.

"Absolutely," I say, still not sure what I'm agreeing to.

To my dismay, I find out when she smugly states, "You do know what I mean is that there will be no sex, right?"

26

A NEW START

CRICKET

"Wait, what?"

It's all I can do to not start laughing.

The look on Landen's face is priceless.

"You heard me," I tell him. Arching a brow, I then ask, "Can you live with no sex?"

Shaking his head, he looks down and says, "God, I don't know."

I roll my eyes. "Please. Like you've never had a dry spell?"

His eyes meet mine again. "I have, of course. And that's fine. I just don't know how I'm supposed to be around *you*, and not be allowed to touch you."

"We can still kiss," I offer helpfully. "And hold hands."

"Er, uh, maybe a few *other* things too?" He waggles his brows.

Damn, he's so handsome, even when he's being silly.

He thinks he's going to have a hard time?

Ha!

I'm going to be dying of unfulfilled lust for this man.

I want to agree to "other things," but that would defeat the whole purpose. The reason for my "no sex" rule is to redo what we moved too quickly on. Since we don't want to totally not see each other, this is really the only part of the past we can change today.

I want us to ultimately reach the same point where we were prior to our problems, before things got stressful for us and consequently bad.

So I'm thinking if we follow this one simple rule, we shouldn't feel trapped or like things are moving too quickly.

It's all about control, and that starts with *self*-control.

Sighing, I maintain, "No sex means no sex, Landen. Not in any way, shape, or form. As you recall, we didn't fuck right away." He groans, and I go on. "We were, though, giving each other orgasms from date number one."

"I know, I know," he concedes, raking his hand through his messy blond hair.

"So no sex is okay with you?"

He doesn't answer, and I prompt, "Landen?"

Reluctantly, he finally replies, "Yes, I'll live with it. But damn."

Damn is right.

Someone has to be strong, though.

I just hope I'm up to the challenge.

Clearing my throat, I tell him, "This will be good in the long run. You'll see."

Dejectedly, he replies, "I guess."

We clearly need a break before we continue our discussion, so I stand and say, "I'm going to grab a glass of ice water. Do you want one?"

He nods. "Yeah, sure, that'd be great. Put extra ice in mine."

That makes me laugh.

I figure the ice water will cool us both down in more ways than one, especially with the "extra ice." I need to cool down because, crap, already knowing I can't have Landen is making me want him even more.

I bet he feels the same way.

He's shifting around uncomfortably over there on the sofa.

So why am I doing this again?

Oh, yes, to better our relationship.

Before I change my mind, I hurry to the kitchen to retrieve the water.

When I return, Landen seems more at peace with the decision.

After I hand him his glass of water, with the extra ice, I sit back down on the chair by the sofa.

Sighing, he says, "So can I ask you out on a proper date now? Since we're being so formal and all."

I take a sip of water, nodding into the glass. "Uh-huh."

Landen clears his throat.

He seems nervous suddenly, and, really, it's cute as hell.

Maybe this is a good idea after all.

I have little butterflies too, of excitement and in anticipation.

"Cricket…" He leans forward. "Would you like to go out to dinner with me tomorrow night? Say, around eight and to someplace nice?"

Oooh, only a one-day wait.

Perfect.

I don't think I could stand days and days away from Landen.

His road trip and our "break"—that's what I'm calling it now—have accounted for more than enough time spent apart.

Breaking into a smile, I tell him, "Yes, I'd love to go to dinner with you."

He raises a brow. "Maybe we can go see a movie afterward?"

I nod excitedly. "That sounds great."

"Then it's a date?"

"It is."

A date I'm beyond excited for.

27

DATE NIGHT

LANDEN

O kay, so I wasn't sold on this taking-a-step-back idea. But I'm slowly warming up to it.

It's Saturday, early in the evening, and I'm getting ready for my "date" with Cricket.

The excitement I feel is palpable.

Though it promises to be hard as hell to not be all over her tonight, I'm up for the challenge. I'm keeping motivated by the thought of how hot it'll be once we do end up back in bed.

"Fuck, man, I'm going to come in two minutes."

I shake my head at my reflection in the mirror, my green eyes laughing at me as I smooth back my hair with some product.

No, you won't, dude.

For her sake.

That's right—I won't.

I'm going to make our first time back to being physical amazing for her.

But for now, we have this date to contend with, so that's where my head is.

It's going to be fun.

I dressed to the nines, in a dark gray suit, white dress shirt, red paisley tie, and shiny-ass shoes.

I'm hoping to knock her socks off.

That's why, once I leave the house, I detour to a local florist to pick up a bouquet of colorful and fragrant flowers.

Oh, and I'm in the Ferrari.

We're going all out here.

I pull into Cricket's driveway a short while later and cut the engine.

Hopping out—*yeah, I feel good*—I bounce up the steps and ring the bell.

Cricket answers the door wearing a sexy formfitting floral dress. She looks stunning. The gauzy fabric hugs her every perfect curve. I also like how her hair is down, but with lots of bounce. It looks like she's curled it at the ends.

"You look gorgeous," I tell her.

"Thanks. You look pretty hot yourself." Her eyes trail up and down my body appreciatively.

I can't help it. That has me thinking dirty thoughts.

Quickly, I hand her the bouquet. "Uh, these are for you."

Taking the flowers, she raises them to her nose and breathes in deeply. "Mmm, they smell fantastic, Landen. Let me just run back in for a sec and put them in some water. Then we can get going."

"Okay."

She doesn't ask me in, nor do I follow.

I already want so badly to hold and touch her.

Why tempt either of us with her bedroom so close by?

She's only going to be a couple of minutes, anyway.

Once Cricket rejoins me on the doorstep, she turns to lock her door.

I try not to check out her ass too much.

But, of course, it's hard and I really don't succeed.

None the wiser of what I'm up to, she spins around to face me.

Innocent look in place, I hold out my arm. "Shall we?" I ask.

Sliding her little hand in the crook of my elbow, she says, "Let's."

She's smiling, and I'm grinning like a fool.

This is turning out to be more fun than I thought it would be.

Taking a step back maybe isn't so bad.

On the way to the restaurant, I tell Cricket that I made a reservation at the very same place we went to on our first date, all those months ago.

"I like that," she says.

"Yes," I concur. "It seemed…appropriate."

"It does," she agrees.

It's going to be like we're reliving—and rewriting—the past. We can keep it the same in some ways but make it better in others.

At the restaurant, we follow the original script and order filet mignon and merlot.

But we don't head out to the desert afterward.

There's a movie, but no fast driving.

There's also lots of hand-holding and a few shy smiles, but no getting each other off in the driver's seat of the Ferrari.

I sort of miss that one.

I remind myself, however, that there will be ample opportunities to relive that experience again down the road. Pun intended.

At the end of the night, there's a good-night kiss on Cricket's front steps.

It's sweet and loving, and it holds the promise of a brighter and better future for us.

And that, my friends, is what is making this all worthwhile.

LANDEN SCORES

CRICKET

Over the next couple of weeks, Landen and I go out on many dates. Dates that pretty much follow the pattern we started that first Saturday night.

There are dinners, movies, pretty flowers from him, and chaste kisses by the door.

Okay, the kisses are becoming less and less chaste as time goes by.

Some are downright smokin' hot.

That's all right, as the increasing heat between us is indicative of our growing relationship.

This experiment is turning out to be a success.

Another victory, occurring in the background for me, but in his professional life for Landen, is that the Wolves are on a tear.

The team is winning games like crazy.

Picking up Sebastian, who now plays at his go-to position of center since Blake is back in the lineup, has proven to be a masterful stroke of genius.

By early April, the regular season is coming to a close, and the Wolves have secured a playoff spot.

Yay!

Everyone is thrilled, so when Ahren asks if I'd like a ticket to go see the last home game of the regular season, I'm all in.

"Hell yes! I'd freaking love to go," I tell her, my enthusiasm bubbling over.

Hey, what can I say?

I love hockey.

I love the Wolves.

And I, of course, love Landen.

Sigh.

Frowning, she says, "Only thing is I was only able to secure one ticket due to the high demand."

"That's fine," I assure her. "I don't mind going alone."

I'm actually more than fine with it, as it will give me an opportunity, like during the first game I ever attended as an employee, to focus on the game.

And, well, on Landen.

Hee hee.

That's exactly what I find myself doing a few hours later.

Seated in a luxury box in the first row, all by myself since the fans in the close by seats wandered off a while ago, I lean forward and watch my man play superb hockey.

We're midway through the second period, and Landen's line is back out on the ice. They've been on fire tonight, having scored twice already.

One goal was a Blake wraparound beauty, and Sebastian put the puck in the net on a sweet breakaway shot.

"Now it's Landen's turn," I mutter, as if saying the words can make it happen.

Hey, they may.

I believe in the power of positive thinking.

The guys are setting up in the other team's zone, passing like they're on a power play.

They're all so good.

Just as I'm thinking that, Landen flips the puck to Sebastian, who settles it down before passing it to Blake.

Landen uses that time to position himself in front of the net.

Blake then fakes a shot to Landen but actually passes the puck to Sebastian.

That throws the defenders off just enough that when Sebastian passes the puck to Landen, no one is there to block his ensuing shot.

He beats the goaltender and scores!

"Yes!" I stand and jump around to the fun song that's played every time the Wolves score.

There's a couple, who has returned from getting food, in the row behind me, so I turn around and high-five them both.

"That's your man, right?" the lady asks, nodding to the ice where Landen is celebrating his goal with his linemates.

I realize then and there that he absolutely is my man—in heart, mind, and soul.

I'm his in those ways too.

Nodding excitedly, I reply, "Yes. Yes, he is."

Winking, she says, "Well, then, looks like you guys have some celebrating to do later tonight."

I just laugh and turn back around.

But you know what?

She's right.

Landen is mine in so many ways, as I am his, but our bodies haven't joined in far too long.

I know then that we've reached the point where it's time.

There are no more misgivings, no more hesitations, and no more fears. It's just me and Landen, in love and for all the right reasons.

So yes, we do have some "celebrating" to do later tonight.

Good thing we have plans to meet up at his house after the game.

We're supposed to watch a movie.

Ha, movie, my ass!

Landen doesn't know it yet, but he's about to do some hot and sexy scoring off the ice…with me.

29

THE BEST KIND OF CELEBRATING

LANDEN

We win the last regular season home game.

I'm thrilled with how my line played.

We scored three of the five Wolves' goals.

Not too shabby, if I do say so myself.

The locker room is raucous.

Everyone is in a fine mood, including me.

Still, I can't wait to shower and dress and head home. I'm supposed to meet up with Cricket so we can watch a movie.

Well, that's the plan, anyway.

I'm so amped up from this stellar game that I wish I could show her how much…in bed.

That'd be a much better—and more fun—way to celebrate.

But alas, it is what it is.

We're still holding off on moving forward physically.

Sighing, I slip off my pads.

Blake, seated next to me on the bench, also undressing, asks, "What's up, Zehner? It sounds like your postgame euphoria is fading already."

"It is," I confess. "But not in the way you're probably thinking."

"Yeah?" He raises a brow. "How so, then?"

I hesitate, then simply tell him the truth. "It's just that Cricket and I are meeting up to hang at my house later, and I fucking wish I could 'celebrate' properly"—I clear my throat meaningfully—"with her."

Blake frowns. "Uh, why can't you?"

Of course he'd be confused. He knows we're taking things slowly after reconnecting, but I've never told a soul that's meant no sex.

When I don't immediately reply, though, he figures it out. "Ahh, you guys are taking the old 'hold off on sexing' slow approach, eh?"

I nod. "Sadly, we are."

Patting my back, he says, "I don't know, man. That works for a while, but maybe it's time to give up on it. You got to get back to doing it someday, right? What better time than after a great game like the one tonight?"

I think it over and realize I completely agree.

"You know what?" I say. "You're fucking right. Why are we still waiting?"

Looking confused, he says, "I don't know, dude. You tell me."

Nodding, I continue, "Maybe I just needed to hear it out loud from someone. I mean, hell, Cricket and I are so much more committed to each other than we were a month ago. There's absolutely no reason to keep holding off."

Blake's eyes widen. "Holy hell, are you saying you haven't fucked your woman in a month?"

I groan. "Ugh, I am saying exactly that. Please don't remind me."

He lets out a low whistle. "Dude, I'm sorry."

"Thanks," I deadpan.

Blake shrugs. "I don't know, man. If I were you, I'd definitely end that shit tonight. Besides celebrating, you sure don't want to wait so long that she forgets how good you can make her feel. It could end up with you guys reaching a point of no return, like sort of friend-zoned forever."

"Shit, I don't know about that," I reply.

But what if he's right?

"Damn it, that's it," I suddenly announce. "I am so fucking out of here."

Blake, knowing what I'll be doing real soon, laughs. "Good decision, man. Now go have some fun."

"Oh, I plan to," I reply.

I take off the rest of my gear so quickly it's not even funny.

I then take the quickest shower ever, get dressed, and practically jog out to my car.

There's an extra step in my stride too.

And why is that?

Because I'm about to give Cricket a night to remember, one she'll never forget.

A NIGHT TO REMEMBER

CRICKET

Landen and I pull up to his house at the same exact time, me entering from one end of his semicircle driveway and he from the other.

We park facing each other.

Then we get out of our cars.

Our eyes meet from afar.

We walk until we're facing one another in the driveway, only a few feet between us.

I see then that we're on the same page.

Decisions have been reached, and it looks like we're thinking the same thing.

There's nothing stopping us now except a few unspoken words.

Let's get this thing moving, my inner voice gripes.

Yes, let's.

Clearing my throat, I say, "That was some game, huh?"

"Did you like it?" Landen asks, tilting his head slightly to one side.

His hair is still a little wet from his shower, making it appear darker than the usual blond shade.

And his eyes, even in the dim lighting, twinkle mischievously.

Smiling, I take a tentative step toward him. "I did enjoy it," I say.

"How much?"

"This much."

I close the gap between us, and then my lips are on his.

Yeah, I'm making the first move, letting him know that I'm ready… for more.

I stand on my tiptoes and wind my arms around his neck.

He deepens our kiss.

I've missed this—the way he tastes, the way he feels, the subtle shift of his body, and the little sigh he lets out as excitement begins to overtake him.

I feel it too, the palpable sexual tension in the air.

It's never left, it was just brewing.

But I'm done with that.

Pulling back, gasping, I ask, "Do you want to go inside?"

Landen raises a brow. "Do you?"

I nod. "Yeah, I do. I think the time has come. We need each other in more ways than just kissing and holding hands."

Laughing, he says, "Damn, woman. You read my mind."

"Did you decide tonight?" I ask, curious as to when he reached his decision.

Nodding, he tells me, "Yes."

"When?"

"After the game. You?"

I smile. "Same."

Landen then sweeps me up in his arms so quickly I barely know what's happening.

Just as fast, he carries me into his house.

"Hmm, this feels very 'caveman' of you," I say, laughing, as he starts up the stairs.

I don't tell him that I love it.

An in-charge Landen is extremely hot.

Holding onto me more tightly, he growls, "You got that right. Just wait till I have you in my bed. And then under me, on top of me, and in every possible way. I've been waiting for this moment for a long time now."

His words send quivers down my spine and to other much lower regions, regions that need his touch, his mouth, his cock.

I let out a groan. "Just hurry, okay?"

He laughs as we reach the landing. "You sound as anxious for this as I am."

"I may be even more anxious," I admit.

Very seriously, and slowing down for a sec, he says, "That is not even possible, babe."

"Hmm, I don't know about that."

Striding quickly again, he mutters, "Yeah, we'll see."

With me securely in his strong arms, Landen kicks open the door to his bedroom and ushers us inside.

His alpha male actions continue as he tosses me onto the bed.

Giggling, I roll over onto my stomach. "I want to watch you undress," I say, my voice thick with lust.

"Your wish is my command," he tells me as he tugs his black long-sleeved tech tee over his head, revealing sculpted abs and a smooth, wide chest. "But…"

"Yes?"

"I get to watch you take your clothes off next."

"Absolutely," I agree, nodding enthusiastically. "Fair is fair, right?"

"You bet it is."

Landen unzips his dark pants and takes them off slowly.

He takes extra time to ditch his shoes and socks, and I grow impatient.

"Just get naked, will you?" I grind out as I rise up to my knees.

"I guess you weren't kidding about being more anxious than I am," he teases.

"I told you," I groan.

I start taking off the Wolves jersey I'm wearing—his number, of course.

Once it's over my head and in my hands, I toss it to him.

He catches it and throws it aside.

Standing in only his boxer briefs, his huge erection on full display, I quickly strip down to just my panties.

Landen's eyes travel over my breasts, down my taut stomach, and then lower still.

"Those"—he nods to my lacy pink undies—"need to go."

"You first," I coo.

With no hesitation, he whips off his boxers, freeing the cock I want so much.

"Mmm…" I purr.

I'm as excited as he is.

Yeah, those lacy panties he wants off so badly are thoroughly soaked.

As I start to pull one side down, I say, "I want you inside me right away. When I say no more waiting, I mean no more waiting."

"Shit, woman, you're not messing around."

"I'm not." I pause on tugging my panties down my legs and warn, "I mean it, Landen. I've waited long enough for this."

"You and me both," he growls. "Now get rid of those panties or I'm ripping them off you."

I giggle. "Oooh, promises, promises."

That's all it takes before Landen descends on me.

Pushing me back onto the bed, he does indeed tear my panties off.

"Good thing I didn't really like those," I tease as he throws the tatters aside.

Landen is too focused on spreading my legs to discern that I'm kidding around, and he tells me, "I'll buy you new ones."

I make him stop for a sec so he can look at me.

With my hand on his chin, I say, "I don't want new ones. I just want you."

Sighing, he leans his forehead to mine as he slowly pushes into me.

"Damn, you feel so good," I gasp.

"Not as good as you feel, beautiful."

We both still then, clearly needing a quiet moment of connection.

But soon what's natural takes over, and Landen begins to move.

I match his every thrust, rolling my hips in the way I know he likes.

"I love you so fucking much," he says. "I'm not afraid to tell you that anymore."

I say it in return, and add, "You're my forever, Landen."

It's true.

No matter what, if there's one thing I've learned, it's that Landen Zehner is the man for me.

I'll never want or love anybody as much as I love and want him.

I know he feels the same way.

And I know he's made peace with that.

As have I.

Sighing contentedly, Landen buries his face in my neck and responds in the way he's best at—loving me with all his body and all his heart and soul.

31

LET'S CLOSE THIS ONE OUT

LANDEN

Cricket tells me I'm her forever, and it gets me to thinking about where we should go from here.

She's my forever too.

I know that now.

That leads me to thinking about what our shared future should hold.

I ponder that thought throughout the night and into the next day.

Even as the first round of hockey playoffs gets underway, Cricket and hockey are the only two things on my mind.

In that order too—my relationship these days comes before all else, even my job that I love.

It's just that I love Cricket more, as it should be.

That's why, after about a week or so, I have an idea of where she and

I should go from here.

I'm waiting for the right time to make my next move, though.

It won't be today.

We have a playoff game tonight.

It's game four against our first round opponents—the San Jose Sharks.

We've done real well against them and are up 3-0 in the series.

They've lost every game so far.

I actually feel kind of bad for them.

Wait, nah, fuck those guys.

The Wolves as a team are unstoppable.

It's hard to beat us right now.

We're firing on all cylinders, as am I.

Later, when I'm in the locker room readying for the game, it's clear the energy is high.

My teammates are wound up, and the crowd out in the seats sounds loud.

I love it, though.

This is what it's all about.

Blake is seated next to me, lacing up his skates.

I'm already dressed, so I'm working on taping my stick.

"You ready for tonight?" he asks, glancing over at me.

I nod. "Yeah. Let's close this one out."

"I think we will," he says. "I have a good feeling."

I finish with my stick and set the tape down on the bench, telling him, "Same here."

We're not the only confident ones in the room. Brent, our captain, wants to give us an inspirational speech before we go out on the ice.

"Gather round," he says, standing before us.

We huddle in.

Clearing his throat, he says, "Guys, we've been here before. And there have been two outcomes. Two years ago, we played as a unit, like the great team we are. We went all the way and won the motherfucking Stanley Cup."

"Hell, yeah!" someone yells out.

"You bet your ass we did," another guy, I think it's Benny, says.

Brent has to stop with all the cheering and whooping and hollering that ensues.

Eventually the room quiets down.

He goes on then, adopting a more somber tone. "Then there was last year. We went out in the second round." Now there's a cacophony of boos and groans. "Okay, okay, enough. Let's not dwell on the negative. But let's not fall apart again. We know we're the best team in the league. Still, even if we win tonight—and we fucking better—we have to get through three more rounds. We do that, boys, and we'll be hoisting up Lord Stanley once again. So let's get out there and do this, yeah?"

The room erupts in shouts and cheers.

I don't think we could be more pumped than we are right now.

When we hit the ice, our fans go crazy.

The arena is rockin' tonight, and we feed off the energy, skating around in the flashing lights with upbeat music blaring.

By the time the first puck drops, the energy is coursing through me, even though I'm on the bench for now.

Brent's top line, composed of him, Nolan, and Benny, is up first.

They don't score, but neither do the Sharks' top line.

Coach Townsend sends my line out next.

Yes!

With Sebastian centering, Blake on right wing, me on the left, and two good defensemen, I feel like one of us is bound to make something happen.

Again, there's just that special feel in the air.

Sure enough, real fucking fast, there's a breakdown in the Sharks' defense, and Sebastian and I enter their zone in a two-on-one situation.

Sebastian passes the puck to me, and I shoot it toward the net.

Holy hell, the motherfucker goes in!

Goal!

"Fuck, yeah!"

I just drew first blood.

That wording turns out to be prophetic, as it's a bloodbath from there. The Wolves score three more unanswered goals in the second period.

By the time the third period rolls around, we go into defensive lockdown mode and the Sharks can't score.

"That's how it's done," Coach Townsend tells us when we're back on the bench. "This is textbook perfect, boys. Keep it up."

We do.

When we win the game, we all jump over the boards and skate over to our goaltender to congratulate him on the shutout.

We also celebrate among ourselves, then we line up for the obligatory handshake with the Sharks' players.

I know some of the guys on the other team, so there's no animosity on my part.

"Hey, no hard feelings," one says. "Congratulations."

I reply, "Thanks, man."

It goes on like that until the lines dwindle down. And then we head off to our respective locker rooms.

It's obviously celebratory in ours, and I'm beyond happy.

I don't share this with anyone, but there's another reason for my joy—the time finally feels right to make my next move with Cricket.

And, man, is it going to be a doozy.

She was up in a luxury box with her friend, Bettina, watching the game.

We're supposed to meet up back at my place in a few.

But I have another idea.

Grabbing my phone from my locker stall, I text Cricket, **Hey, you feel like going out and celebrating tonight?**

She writes back, **Yeah, sure. What do you have in mind?**

Me: How about something we haven't done in a while?

Cricket: Er, okay, I think. But I may need more details before I say yes.

Me: Right, lol. Anyway, I thought it might be fun to go play some blackjack. It's been a while. What do you think?

Cricket: Sure, I'm up for that. It sounds fun. Do you mean we'll go to the same private VIP room where we first met?

Me: You know me so well. I was thinking exactly that.

Cricket: Cool, let's do it. Bettina was planning on dropping me off at your house since she drove tonight, but I can just send her on her way and meet you outside the locker room. We can head straight over to the casino.

Me: Perfect, babe. Just give me about twenty minutes.

We wrap up, and I start taking off my equipment.

Cricket has no idea, but I have an idea for a bet I'm going to make with her tonight, one that I absolutely *must* win.

The future of us depends on it.

32

WHAT IS MY MAN UP TO?

CRICKET

As I slip my phone back into my purse, I have one thing on my mind—*What is my man up to?*

I mean, I'm more than willing to go out and celebrate, and I always have fun beating Landen's ass in cards—*hee hee*—but I sense there's something more at play with this outing.

I share my plans and my thoughts with Bettina before we leave the luxury box, and she says, "Who knows? But I'm sure if Landen is up to something, it's nothing bad."

I wave my hand around. "Oh, no, I know that. I just wish I had some idea of what he has in mind."

After thinking it over, she says, "Well, your birthday is coming up soon, right? Maybe he's planning on surprising you with a cake."

Frowning, I reply, "No, I don't think it's that. My birthday isn't till

May, and that's almost a month away."

Clearly at a loss, Bettina shrugs. "I don't know, then, hon."

We drop the subject, and I resign myself to the fact I just need to go with the flow and quit trying to guess what Landen has up his sleeve. Like Bettina said, I'm sure it's nothing bad. I'm just an overly curious person, I guess.

With the subject dropped, Bettina and I say our goodbyes, and she takes off.

I head downstairs to the locker room, where the security guy on the elevator nods to me, having recognized that I'm allowed to go down to that level.

As indicated in his texts, Landen is waiting for me outside the locker room double doors. He looks extremely happy, and I have the feeling it's not simply due to the great game he and the team just played.

Still, I am quick to acknowledge the performance with a loose hug.

"Hey," I say, stepping back. "You guys kicked some incredible ass out there tonight."

Smoothing down the front of his hunter green dress shirt, the color of which really brings out the pretty sage shade of his eyes, he says, "We did. It felt good too. We were firing on all cylinders."

"Wolves all the way," I chime in, pumping my fist in the air. "Yay!"

That makes Landen chuckle. "Babe, you really are the best."

"Why, thank you," I say, batting my eyelashes coquettishly.

I love playing around with Landen. He's not only hot and sexy; he has an amazing playful side.

Holding out his arm for me to take, he says, "Shall we go?"

"Yes, let's do it." I wind my arm within his and add, "By the way, I can't wait to beat you in cards tonight."

Landen laughs jovially. "Confident, aren't we?"

Bumping his leg with my hip, I say, "You know it."

Outside in the players' parking lot, we hop into his Ferrari.

We're then off to the Vegas Strip, where I plan to not only win *all* the money but also I'll finally find out what Landen is really up to with this impromptu gambling date.

33

UPPING THE ANTE

LANDEN

We arrive at the casino where Cricket and I first met.

I've chosen it so I can "up the ante."

We head inside through the back entrance, and security whisks us to the VIP room.

This is all mainly so I don't have to stop and sign autographs or take selfies with excited fans.

I'm always accommodating, but tonight I have a bigger purpose and I need to focus.

I have to chuckle, as Cricket still has no idea what I'm up to.

I think she may suspect something is in the works, though.

Still, she has no clue as to what it could be.

I can't wait to surprise her.

She will be floored.

Smiling discreetly, I take her hand, and we walk over to our favorite blackjack table.

Bettina is obviously not working, as she was at the game with Cricket. There's an older dude here tonight, dealing the cards.

As Cricket and I take side-by-side seats at the table, I give her a quick peck on the cheek.

"Good luck," I say.

"Ha!" She laughs. "I'm not going to need it. As you are well aware, I'm already quite lucky."

"We'll see," I cryptically comment.

There's a new game starting, so we're able to get in on it.

A waitress swings by to see if we'd like anything to drink.

"Just a soda water," Cricket tells her.

I ask for the same.

I want to be as coherent as possible when I spring my surprise.

Maybe if all goes well, we'll have champagne afterward.

But for now, we play cards.

I win the first game, but the guy on my left is victorious the next.

There are five people playing initially, but eventually we're down to three.

I win a couple more rounds, and Cricket wins a total of five times.

She's on a hot streak tonight.

It's daring for me to even think about the bet I'm planning.

But hey, I'm a risk-taker.

Besides, when the guy on my left leaves, I like my chances.

"Guess it's down to just the two of us," Cricket says.

Winking over at her, I reply, "That's okay. That's my favorite way to play with you."

"I agree," she replies in a sultry tone. "It's mine too."

We both clearly mean more than cards, but cards are what are on the table right now…in more ways than one.

The dealer passes out our next hands.

I check mine—I have a king of hearts and a jack of clubs.

That's twenty.

This is really good.

Now is definitely the time to make my move.

I'm upping the ante for sure now.

But I'm hedging my bet.

Looking over at Cricket, I notice her checking her cards discreetly.

She smiles.

Hmm, I wonder what she has.

It could be twenty-one, but I doubt it.

Clearing my throat, I ask her, "Are you up for one of our little side wagers?"

Peering over at me with a smug-as-fuck expression, she replies, "For sure. Let's do it."

I qualify, "We'll keep it a secret till a winner is declared, yeah?"

She nods. "Like usual, yes."

I then remark, "You sound pretty confident, babe."

Snickering, she says, "That's because I am confident, Landen."

Shit, she is.

Now I'm really wondering what she has.

If it's twenty-one, I'm fucked.

Both of us hold, so it must be something good.

I had better fucking win.

The dealer flips his cards—he has eighteen.

He holds.

Cricket and I look at each other.

"Ladies first," I say.

"Fine."

She's damn confident as she flips her cards over.

But I'm the one smiling when I see she has a king and a nine—that's only nineteen.

I win!

I flip my cards over and smirk my ass off.

Cricket rolls her eyes at me. "Okay, okay, what have I lost this time?"

"Maybe nothing," I reply, shrugging. "With what I'm about to ask for, I think we're both going to come out winners."

She's peering at me intently now, her azure eyes filled with curiosity.

"So what is it?" she asks. "Tell me what you want from me."

"Among a lot of things," I say in a rush of words, "I want you to marry me."

Her eyes grow wide, and the dealer chuckles.

"What did you just say?" Cricket rasps.

"You heard me. Should I drop down to one knee and make it more official?"

I don't wait for her answer, I just do it.

I ask her again for her hand in marriage.

"I don't have a ring yet," I explain. "But we can fix that real soon. That is, if you say yes."

Softly and with happy tears in her eyes, she tells me what I long to hear. "Yes."

Teasing, I cup my hand behind my ear. "What's that, Cricket? I'm not sure I heard."

"Oh, stop being silly," she pshaws. "I said yes, I'll marry you."

I stand then, readying to hug and kiss her, but I hesitate. "Wait.

You're not just saying yes because of the bet, right?"

With a mischievous glint in her eyes, she says, "Well, I do always make good on my wagers."

"Hey!"

She starts laughing and tugging me to her. "Come here, you. You know I'm just kidding."

"Yeah, I do."

I do know it.

That's why I just crash my lips down on hers.

It's our first kiss as an engaged couple.

And does it ever feel good.

There's no panic, no reservations, no second-guessing, nothing but pure love.

34

I DIDN'T SEE THIS ONE COMING

CRICKET

Okay, I knew Landen was up to something.

But I sure didn't see this one coming.

He wants me to marry him?

He sure didn't have to engage me—no pun intended—in one of his side bets to get me to say yes to that.

But he needs to hear it.

So, choking up, I murmur, "Yes."

He pretends not to be clear on my answer, cupping his ear. "What's that, Cricket? I'm not sure I heard."

"Oh, stop being silly," I reply. "I said yes, I'll marry you."

He stands but then hesitates. "Wait. You aren't just saying yes because of the bet, right?"

Okay, now it's my turn to tease him.

Tapping my chin, I say, "Well, I do always make good on my wagers."

"Hey!"

I smile, pulling him to me. "Come here, you. You know I'm just kidding."

Sheepishly, he admits, "Yeah, I do."

He wastes no time in kissing me then.

And wow, what a kiss it is!

Even the dealer lets out a low whistle.

At last, we break apart.

With his forehead pressed to mine, Landen asks, "Do you want to cash out and go home?"

"Yes," I say. "But to whose home?"

He straightens, placing his hands on my shoulders.

With much seriousness in his tone, he says, "They'll both be *our* homes soon, right?"

I nod. "That's true."

They will be once we're married.

Holy crap!

That's when it really hits me—*I'm marrying Landen freaking Zehner!*

It makes me feel so good to know we're engaged and our lives are now intertwined more than ever.

Since I can't wait to get Landen to *any* house at this point, simply so I can attack him and devour his hot ass, I suggest the closer one. "Let's go to your place."

He raises a brow. "You mean *our* place."

"Yes, yes"—I laugh—"our place that happens to be in your name."

"For now," he replies. "It's in my name only for the time being,

Cricket."

Wow, this is what "real" feels like.

This is what "happiness" feels like.

And this is what "forever" feels like.

EPILOGUE

FOREVER

LANDEN

The very next day, Cricket and I agree on a reputable local jewelry store where we can pick out her engagement ring.

I considered going on my own, but it's not like the ring needs to be a surprise.

No, I think my impromptu-side-wager proposal checked that box.

Cricket told me she never saw it coming.

I'm sure she didn't.

But it worked out beautifully and fit us as a couple.

We like to do things differently.

We may hit a snag sometimes, but we work it out.

At the jewelers, Cricket chooses something called a radiant cut diamond and decides to have it set in platinum.

That's fine with me.

We pick it up from the store a few days later.

When we reach the car and pop open the little dark green velvet box to take a second look, I note, "It sure is sparkly."

"It is," she agrees, peering down at the ring with a smile on her face.

I can tell she loves it, so I ask, "Are you going to put it on now?"

She looks up at me. "Should I?"

I'm about to say yes, but then I have an idea. "Are you okay with waiting a few more hours? I want us to do something this evening."

"And this 'something' would involve the ring?" she asks.

"It would. Or rather, it will." I touch her arm. "So are you okay with waiting a short while longer before you put it on?"

Nodding, she gives me the ring.

Excellent!

My plan is set in motion then.

And the next few hours go by surprisingly fast.

Once darkness falls, I take Cricket out to the desert where she and I drove the Ferrari as fast as we dared the night of our first date.

It's also where we made a bet, one that I won and asked her to not see other people.

I wanted her to give me a real chance.

And she did.

Oh, did she ever.

And though we hit a rough patch due to the pressure my winning ultimately put on us, it all worked out okay.

We've come out more solid in the end.

That's why my plan is that I want to propose again, officially with the ring, out here in the desert, where it's just Cricket and me under a vast night sky filled with a million twinkling stars.

"It's so pretty out here at night," she says as I pull to the side of the road, same spot as before.

"It always is," I agree.

When we get out of the car, Cricket shivers and wraps her arms around her pink sweater-clad torso.

The desert is a little cool tonight, and her sweater isn't heavy, so I offer her my jacket. "Here, put this on. Those leggings are really thin. I know from experience." I wink at her. "From all the times I've taken them off you."

Laughing, she slips the jacket on. "Mmm, yes. Oh, and this is much better with the jacket. Thanks."

"Of course, sweetheart."

I'm in a button-down shirt and jeans, so I'm plenty warm. I run a little hotter than Cricket, anyway.

That's why I then wrap her up in my arms, warming her further.

"I love you," I murmur, kissing her cheeks one at a time. "You know that, right?"

She leans back slightly. "I do, Landen. I love you too."

"I know, sweetheart."

Letting her go, I drop down to one knee.

The time is right.

There's a big orange moon up in the sky, much like our first night out here, and it's casting just enough light to set the scene for romance.

Taking out the little ring box I had Cricket give me in the jeweler's parking lot, I pop open the lid.

The ring shimmers and sparkles in the moonlight.

On bended knee, I ask, "Will you marry me, Cricket?"

"Yes, I will."

"And now I'm going to do the rest of this right." I take the ring from the box and slide it onto the ring finger of her left hand.

I then stand and kiss her like I mean it.

I do mean it.

My love for this woman knows no bounds.

It's as endless as the starry night sky above us.

We make no plans for when we'll walk down the aisle.

But we know it'll happen not too far in the future.

Maybe there will be a bet involved.

Or maybe there won't be.

I kind of think there will, though.

Whatever the case, we'll do it our way, in our own time.

We're unconventional like that.

We're Landen and Cricket.

And we're together—tonight, tomorrow, and forever.

THE END

Up next in the bestselling Boys of Winter hockey romance series
of interconnected standalones is Sebastian's story, **DARE ON ICE**,
releasing December 2021

And in the bestselling Men of Fall football romance novels, look for
Zane's story, *Down by Contact*, set to release in June 2021

ABOUT THE AUTHOR

S.R. Grey is a USA Today Bestselling Author of the popular Boys of Winter hockey books and Men of Fall football novels. Both series can be read in any order or as standalones. Other New Adult and Romantic Suspense works of hers include the Judge Me Not books, the Promises series, the Inevitability duology, A Harbour Falls Mystery trilogy, and the Laid Bare series of novellas.

Ms. Grey resides in Pennsylvania. When not writing, she can be found reading, traveling, running, or cheering for her hometown sports teams, sometimes all at the same time.

Author Website (stop on by to see how pretty it is):
http://srgrey.com/

S.R. Grey's Facebook page is a hoot:
http://www.facebook.com/SRGrey

S.R. Grey's Facebook Reading Group is even MORE fun:
https://www.facebook.com/groups/SRGreyHardAbsandHotBooks/

S.R. Grey on Twitter (for the random tweets):
https://twitter.com/AuthorSRGrey

S.R. Grey on Instagram for the riveting pics (well, she thinks so):
http://instagram.com/authorsrgrey

S.R. Grey Goodreads Author page: http://www.goodreads.com/author/show/6433082.S_R_Grey

Wait!

It's not over yet.

Read the first chapter of **Forward Progress**, the first standalone novel in the bestselling *Men of Fall* football romance series, where football meets romance.

Chapter One:
Leaving Las Vegas

Graham

I hesitate, my pen hovering over the yellow sheet of legal paper on my desk as I contemplate what to write.

What am I doing?

I'm making a list of what I'd like to achieve throughout the second half of this year. But damn, it's no easy task.

I want to get this done, though. The rehab I went through a couple of years ago made me a big believer in things like setting goals and writing out lists.

My brain is usually racing when I write these kinds of things. I have so much to get down on paper that my pen moves too fast, leaving my sentences a jumbled blur of words I have to decipher later.

Today, however, I've got nothing.

Maybe because all my most recent goals have been achieved…and therefore checked off.

Like this one—I wanted to have my own gym business *and* make it a raging success.

Check, check.

Both of those objectives have been achieved.

And then there's my ongoing goal of always trying to give back and help others.

Check that off too.

I'm still an active sponsor for Narcotics Anonymous, even if it is only for one guy these days—Las Vegas Wolves hockey player Benjamin Perry.

Still counts, though, right?

Ah, but Perry hardly needs me anymore. He's doing really well on his own.

In the past, I always had my sister, Chloe, to worry about. She wasn't in NA or anything, but she had her share of troubles in the relationship department. Seemed I was always swooping in to rescue her.

But she met and married someone great—Dylan Culderway, another hockey player I'm friends with. Chloe now has a calm and happy life. She and Dylan even have a baby on the way.

Fuck, I can't wait to be an uncle.

I spend a few minutes wondering if their baby will have dark blonde hair and cerulean blue eyes like my sister and I do, or if she'll have brown eyes and dark hair like Dylan.

Oh hell, I'm just stalling.

"Get to work on that list, Graham," I mutter to myself to conjure up some motivation. "There has to be at least *one* important thing you have yet to achieve."

And there is.

But it's the one goal I've resisted writing down, on this or any prior lists.

Maybe because this goal is the most important of all and putting it down on paper gives it life. That means it's something I'll *have* to achieve.

No excuses.

"Just write it down, dumbass," I hiss. "Do it. It's the one thing you've wanted more than anything these past three years."

What is this big goal?

It's to play professional football again.

Shit, it's out there now.

I mean, I can't unthink it.

"But what if I *can't* play like I once did?" I whisper, like that would be the worst thing in the world.

Hell, it would.

Other thoughts race through my mind…

What if my once promising football career is really and truly over?

What if I'm washed up?

Do you see now why I'm afraid to write down this goal?

"But you were good." I touch pen to paper, willing my hand to move. "No, you were fucking great, Graham Tettersaw."

It's true, I was. I had a completion percentage in the 65 percent range, and I passed for over 3000 yards every season I played.

I also averaged 30+ touchdowns a year, meaning I was rarely intercepted.

Not to mention, the fans fucking loved me.

I was a god, damn it!

But then I got hurt, and a god I was no more. I was just a man, a man with a blown knee and a crappy attitude. Hence the prescription drug addiction. I just didn't care.

The team I was playing for at the time—the Arizona Cardinals—cut my ass. Doctors, really good ones, told me I'd never play again.

Down in the dumps about, well, just about everything, I developed that nasty painkiller addiction.

That led me to NA.

It worked, and I got clean and sober.

I still am—painkiller-free for over three years now.

That's why I like to give back as a sponsor. It's the least I can do. I believe if I can overcome addiction, anyone can.

"So what would everyone you've helped want you to do now?" I ask myself out loud.

I know the answer. It's simple, really.

They'd want me to believe in myself as much as I believed in them.

That finally gets the pen moving and I write down the one goal that means the world to me—I want to play professional football again.

Shit, that feels good.

On a roll, I jot down another—I'd like to be picked up by a good team.

Problem with that is I'm thirty years old. I'll actually be thirty-one this September, which is only four months away.

There's not much call for a quarterback in his early thirties, especially if he's been out of the game for a few years.

But I have a few things going for me…

I've kept myself in great shape. And I just landed a slick new agent.

I made that move after I discovered the one I had the past few years wasn't even trying anymore.

This new one, Jock Sosarelli, is fantastic. He represents a ton of sports figures, including some of my hockey pals. Brent Oliver is one of his clients. He's the biggest star for the Las Vegas Wolves, so that's something right there.

Jock is good, really good.

A middle-aged former professional athlete, the guy knows sports. Jock used to play baseball, like a hundred years ago.

Okay, not that long ago, but I like to tell him that.

Good thing he takes it well.

Another reason why Jock is a good fit for me is because an injury ended his career too. He understands the perils I face. That's probably why he was quick to pick me up as a new client. I think he'd like to see me get the second chance he never did.

My cell phone rings, breaking me from my reverie. And wouldn't you know it, it's Jock. He wants to FaceTime, so this must be good news.

Leaning back in the chair in my office, I hold the phone up.

Jock's silver-streaked black hair and smiling mug fill the screen.

"Hey, what's up?" I say.

"A lot," he replies. "And you're going to love this news, Tettersaw."

"Hmm…" I'm curious, but first I feel compelled to remind him, "You can call me Graham, you know?"

"Eh, sure, whatever you say, Tettersaw."

I chuckle.

So much for that.

Last names are Jock's shtick. Though I've noticed when shit gets real, he uses first names.

"Okay, so what's this great news, Jock?"

Sliding his reading glasses up the bridge of his nose, he peers down at what looks like a contract of some sort. I've seen enough, I should know.

My heart starts beating like crazy. *Could this be a football deal?* I want this so badly.

As my excitement builds, he says, "I think I have something in the works for you."

I have a shot at making a team? I need to know, but I'm afraid to ask.

But I must.

So, slowly, I murmur, "What kind of something are we talking about here?"

Without looking up from what just has to be a contract, Jock says, "There's a team expressing great interest in you, Graham."

Whoa, he just used my first name. This is the real deal. And that is definitely a contract in his hands.

Fuck.

He goes on, "This team would like to fly you out to their mini-camp. It's going on right now. You could run some reps so they can see you in action, verify your arm is still strong—"

"It is," I interrupt.

Jock talks right over me. "—*and* to make certain your knee is no longer a problem."

I assure him my knee's not an issue at all, and he says, "Good. We'll have to move fast then, if you're interested."

Am I interested?

Is he crazy?

Laughing, I assure him, "I'm interested, Jock. Fuck, trust me, I am."

"Good to hear. If this team likes what they see"—he picks up the contract and waves it in the air, making the screen blur—"they're prepared to follow through on a more-than-fair offer."

My breath catches in my throat. Could this be the shot I've been wishing and hoping for? Hell, the ink's not even dry on my list of new goals.

This is almost too good to be true, though.

So, erring on the side of caution, I inquire, "Which team are we talking about here, Jock?"

He replies "the Columbus Comets," and my heart sinks.

I knew this was too perfect.

"Did you say the Comets?" I verify.

"Yes, the new team in Columbus, Ohio."

I blow out a disappointed breath. "I know who you mean. They're part of the new football league. The one created just last year."

"Yes, that's them," Jock confirms.

"They're not the NFL, Jock."

Instantly, he snaps, "No, Tettersaw, they're not. But we're still talking about a damn fine opportunity."

He's not entirely wrong.

I'm just torn.

Last year, a two-country league emerged. Comprised of twenty-six teams in the US and Canada, this start-up organization managed to cobble together a surprisingly successful inaugural season.

So, yeah, it's not all bad.

"You're right, Jock," I concede, sighing. "But just so you know, the Comets are *not* my first choice by any means."

He chuckles. "I'm sure they're not, Graham. But there's a lot of chatter that this new league is the league of the future. Think about it for a minute. We're talking fan bases in *two* countries. There's so much room for expansion. This is a good opportunity, my man. And the terms the Comets have outlined for you, if you were to be picked up, are more than equitable."

"Ah, hell,"—I run my hand down my face—"I just don't know."

Blowing out a clearly frustrated breath, Jock says, "I'm going to lay it on the line for you. You're not getting any younger, Tettersaw. That means you can pretty much forget about making a comeback in the NFL. The way that league see things, you had your chance. Now you're just a washed-up former star who carries around a history of painkiller problems."

"Hey!" I bristle. "I only had that problem once. And it was ages ago. I've come a long way since then."

Jock is unruffled, no surprise there.

"Hey, hey, don't get pissed at me. I'm just telling you the way it is. You want a chance to start as a quarterback at the professional level?"

"Yes, of course I do," I snap.

"Well, then this is it, my man. To be honest, this could be an opportunity for you to really shine."

"Ha-ha." I chuckle. "You mean like a comet?"

Jock laughs.

He likes that.

"Yes, I guess you could say that," he says.

"Hell, what the fuck do I have to lose?" I say. "Tell the Comets I'm interested, okay?"

"You got it. And for the record, you're making the right decision, Graham."

"I hope so," I mumble.

He ignores me and goes on. "I'll fax you the contract in a few minutes. You can look it over thoroughly. I'll also book you a flight to Columbus."

"Perfect, thanks."

After we wrap up, I place my cell on the desk. And then I think about what this means.

Following some serious contemplation, I begin to feel pretty good about this opportunity. I mean, hell, everything Jock said to me is true. The Columbus Comets may not be part of the NFL, but they're no chumps. And, more importantly, they're offering me a chance to play professional football again.

So Columbus, Ohio, hmm…

That's a long way from Las Vegas, where I currently live. But this could be the push I've needed to start a life of my own.

I'm not talking football anymore. No. These past few years I've spent so much time helping others that I've kind of neglected my own self. Even my sister tells me that.

And it's true. I have no wife, no girlfriend, no kids, and, outside of the gym business, no real life.

Shit.

Picking up the pen, I add one more goal to my list—*leave Las Vegas and start a new life.*

Yeah, I like that one.

Because, just like in football, in order to win, you have to have forward progress.

Continue reading *Forward Progress* on Amazon....
Amazon: https://amzn.to/2s4zM3W

www.ingramcontent.com/pod-product-compliance
Lightning Source LLC
Chambersburg PA
CBHW020411210626
46816CB00006BB/2230